The door chimed and Laurel glanced up to welcome her next customer

The smile forming on her face froze the minute she saw him.

Corb Lambert.

She'd heard he'd been out of hospital for several weeks now. She'd wondered if maybe he would phone her when he was finally released, and when he hadn't, she'd told herself she shouldn't be surprised. He'd been through a lot physically, and had lost a brother besides. He wouldn't have time or inclination to think about the woman he'd charmed during the week before his accident.

But now he was here, and clearly his smile and the twinkle in his eyes hadn't been damaged one bit. "Hello, sugar. Looks like Coffee Creek got a whole lot sweeter since the last time I was in town."

She smiled, thinking he was feeding her the same line on purpose. But when she glanced up at him, she saw no spark of recognition in his eyes. "Corb?"

He looked puzzled. Then he frowned. "Have we met before?"

Dear Reader,

Welcome to Coffee Creek, Montana, the setting of my new series for Harlequin American Romance. You're about to meet the Lamberts—a family of ranchers and cowboys who own the largest spread in Bitterroot County, all controlled by matriarch Olive Lambert. Olive would like to control more than just the operations of the ranch—she also has ideas about what jobs her children should work and who they should marry. Does mother know best? I'll let you be the judge.

One of the pleasures of writing a family saga is creating the setting for the stories. In this case I took a real town name—Coffee Creek, Montana—nudged it a little in the southwesterly direction, made it the head of fictional Bitterroot County and decked it out with interesting establishments like the Cinnamon Stick Café and the Lonesome Spur Saloon. There's a two-story brick courthouse in the center of town, next to the post office and library. If you'd like to see the pictures that inspired the setting and stories, you can visit my storyboards on www.pinterest.com under CJ_Carmichael.

Once you've soaked in the ambience of the setting, please go ahead and meet our first hero and heroine of the series—Corb Lambert and Laurel Sheridan. Their story was so much fun to write. Just imagine you had a whirlwind courtship with a fellow, were sure you had fallen in love, and then he had a head injury and forgot he'd ever met you. What happens next? Just keep reading....

C.J. Carmichael

www.cjcarmichael.com

Remember Me, Cowboy

C.J. CARMICHAEL

HARLEQUIN®

entertain, enrich, inspire™

Recycling programs
for this product may
not exist in your area.

ISBN-13: 978-0-373-75438-0

REMEMBER ME, COWBOY

Copyright © 2013 by Carla Daum

This edition published by arrangement with Harlequin Books S.A.

For questions and comments about the quality of this book, please contact us at CustomerService@Harlequin.com.

www.Harlequin.com

Printed in U.S.A.

ABOUT THE AUTHOR

Hard to imagine a more glamorous life than being an accountant, isn't it? Still, C.J. Carmichael gave up the thrills of income tax forms and double-entry bookkeeping when she sold her first book in 1998. She has now written more than twenty-eight novels for Harlequin, and invites you to learn more about her books, see photos of her hiking exploits and enter her surprise contests at www.cjcarmichael.com.

Books by C.J. Carmichael

HARLEQUIN AMERICAN ROMANCE

HARLEQUIN SUPERROMANCE

*Harts of the Rodeo
**Return to Summer Island
***Three Good Men
‡The Fox & Fisher Detective Agency

This is for the Happy Bookers, with whom I've shared many evenings of good conversations about books and life, bottles of wine and wedges of cheese: Cheryl, Marg, Mary, Mary-Lou, Nancy, Rhonda, Shelli, Sunita and Susan.

Prologue

Where was the groom? Laurel checked her watch, not sure whether to feel annoyed or worried. Her best friend Winnie Hays should have been marching down the aisle of the Coffee Creek United Church ten minutes ago.

As young girls, growing up together in a Montana farming community about an hour from Coffee Creek, she and Winnie had planned their wedding days down to the color of the flowers and the flavor of the cake. Actually, Winnie had planned, and Laurel had gone along with her, claiming to want whatever it was that Winnie wanted.

For the longest time their friendship had worked that way. Winnie decided to take swimming lessons, so Laurel did, too. Winnie started dating a boy, so Laurel dated his best friend. After they'd finished high school and Winnie applied to college in Great Falls, no one had been surprised when Laurel decided to study at the University of Great Falls, too.

Only after they'd earned their undergraduate degrees had Laurel finally realized that she yearned for something Winnie didn't—to leave Montana. So, scared to death but determined, she moved to New York City on her own to pursue her dream of a career in magazine publishing.

To her credit, Winnie never tried to talk her out of her decision. "You have to go for it, Laurel. Or you'll always wonder *what if...*"

Good advice. From a good friend.

And now, three years later, on what should have been the happiest day of Winnie's life, the bride was starting to panic. "I don't understand. Brock promised he'd be *early.*"

The ceremony had been scheduled to start at three o'clock. Fifteen minutes to the hour a dark sedan had arrived from Coffee Creek Ranch driven by Brock's eldest brother, B.J. Dark-haired B.J., with his noble high forehead and chiseled features, had escorted his mother, Olive, into the church.

Olive, still pretty at sixty, her petite figure showcased in an ivory-colored, raw silk suit, had walked proudly on her son's arm as they made their way to the front pew. Having met her several times now during her week in Coffee Creek, Laurel still found it difficult to believe that this diminutive, soft-spoken woman ran the biggest ranch in all of Bitterroot County.

That arrival had been twenty-five minutes ago. Now the church was packed with invited guests and the organist had just started through her repertoire for the third time.

"This is *so* not a good sign." Winnie grabbed bunches of white satin, hitching up her dress so she could stand on a chair for a better view down the street. "Where the hell are they?"

"They" included not only the groom, Brock Lambert, but the middle Lambert son, Corb, who was the best man—and no doubt about that in Laurel's mind, though she'd only known him a week—and the driver, Jackson Stone.

Jackson was the quiet one. So far Laurel had been unable to engage him in any conversation lasting more than five minutes, so it was only thanks to Winnie that she knew he'd come to the Lambert's ranch as a foster child when he was thirteen. Apparently he'd taken to ranch life so well he was now considered part of the family.

"What time did Corb say they left?" Winnie asked, though she already knew the answer.

"Thirty-five minutes ago." Laurel bit her lower lip anxiously. The drive from the Coffee Creek Ranch to town normally took fifteen minutes. No higher mathematics degree was required to figure out they should be here by now.

"What's happened…?" Winnie spoke softly, her gaze still fixed to the street.

"Don't worry," Laurel soothed. "Could be they ran out of gas or had a flat."

"Or maybe they got halfway here only to realize that Corb forgot the ring." Cassidy Lambert smirked. As the only girl in a family of four boys—if you counted Jackson, and most people did—she didn't faze easily. Or conform. She'd agreed to be Winnie's bridesmaid on the condition that she would not wear high heels. "It has to be running shoes or cowboy boots," she'd dictated. "Take your pick."

Which explained the cream-colored boots in butter-soft ostrich leather that she was swinging as she sat on her perch on the ledge of the same window that Winnie was peering out of.

"But if they've been held up," Winnie reasoned, correctly in Laurel's mind, "why haven't they called?"

That was the unanswerable question. One of three men might have forgotten to charge his phone last night. But all three? Hearing tears in Winnie's voice, Laurel stepped forward to urge her off the chair.

"You're making me dizzy up there. Here, sit for a while. You heard Olive say that this would be the first time one of her boys had been to church in a decade. Maybe they got lost and, being men, won't stop for directions."

Laurel generally counted on humor in moments of tension. And she was rewarded with a wisp of a smile, before Winnie's faced creased with worry again.

The fact was, no one could miss the church in Coffee Creek. The white steeple made it the tallest building in a town of about fifteen hundred people. Damn those Lambert men. How could they do this to Winnie? They better have one hell of a good excuse for being so late.

"I'll call *them*." Cassidy jumped softly to the wooden floor. "I'll go get my phone."

As soon as she'd left for the minister's office where they'd stowed their personal effects, Winnie let out a small moan.

"I can't stand this anymore. I've been dying to tell Brock, but you'll have to be the first to know."

"Know what?" Long familiarity with her friend's dramatic streak meant Laurel didn't overreact. She frowned at a scuff on her imitation Valentino pumps, then tried rubbing it off with her thumb.

"Maybe you should sit down. I don't want you fainting or anything."

"Fat chance, Winnie. I am *not* the fainting kind." But she abandoned the scuff. This actually sounded serious.

"I called Brock at the crack of dawn today and told him to get to the church early. That there was something I needed to tell him before the ceremony."

"So you decided to come clean about your criminal record? Good call."

Winnie didn't even crack a smile. "I'm serious, Laurel. I should have told him earlier, but I was in shock myself."

Laurel didn't interrupt this time when Winnie paused. She just waited for her friend to find the right words.

"I'm pregnant."

Laurel could feel her mouth drop open. She couldn't help it. Those were *not* the right words she'd been expecting to hear. "Holy cow. Really?"

"Yes. Two months along, I figure—"

Winnie stopped talking as the door opened. Cassidy was back, cell phone in hand, frowning.

"Brock isn't answering." She punched another button. "I'll try Corb."

No one spoke. The relentless repitition of "Ode to Joy" was getting on Laurel's nerves.

"Damn." Cassidy disconnected the call after reaching the answering service. Next she tried Jackson's number. Again, no one picked up. "If this is some sort of prank, I'm going to kill them."

But Laurel could see the worry in Cassidy's deep green eyes. She was scared. So was Winnie. Her face had gone whiter than the fabric of her wedding gown, making her brown eyes seem almost as black as her hair.

Winnie glanced out the window again. "Someone's coming! I think it's Jackson's SUV...."

Cassidy peered over her shoulder. "No. It's a County Sheriff vehicle."

The three women exchanged looks, no one saying what they were all thinking. This couldn't be good. Laurel's pulse thumped crazily in her throat as she watched the driver park in front of the church. A long-legged woman dressed in uniform, dark hair worn in a long braid to accommodate her hat, stepped out to the street. She glanced left, right, then seemed to take a deep breath before heading inside the church.

"Who was that?" Laurel wondered.

"Sheriff Savannah Moody." Winnie's voice was unnaturally low. "She's a good friend of Brock's. We were going to invite her to the wedding, but he said there was bad blood between her and B.J. I don't know the details."

Laurel's mind went blank, refusing to speculate on the reasons for the sheriff's unexpected appearance. Instead, she thought of the day, a week ago, when she'd arrived at the airport in Billings, having spent most of a day traveling to Montana from New York City.

Winnie had been called in for an unexpected dress fitting and so she'd sent the best man to collect Laurel. Corb Lambert, brother of the groom. "He'll be the cowboy with a dimple in his left cheek," was all Winnie wrote in her hurried text message.

Laurel hadn't seen him at first. She was worried

about her bag, which hadn't appeared on the carousel, even though most of her fellow passengers on Delta 4608 had claimed their luggage and departed the airport at least five minutes ago.

"Please don't let them have lost my suitcase," she pleaded with the airline gods. Besides her clothes for the week, she stood to lose her bridesmaid gown and Winnie and Brock's wedding gift.

And then she saw them both, in the same second. The brown, beaten suitcase with the pink ribbon tied around the handle. And the cowboy striding toward her with a grin and a sparkle to his eye that made her automatically pat her hair and suck in her tummy.

"Sugar?" He walked right up to her. "If you're Laurel Sheridan I think Coffee Creek is about to become a whole lot sweeter."

A corny line, but, oh, how her heart had pounded.

As it was pounding now, in a much less pleasant way.

Laurel squeezed Winnie's hand, staying close to her friend, who'd started to tremble. They followed Cassidy out the door of the antechamber into the vestibule. Two wide doors stood open to the church where all the guests awaited. Chatter filled the air, along with the Beethoven.

And then, abruptly, the organ stopped and everyone turned, expecting to see the bride. A collective gasp washed over the room when Sheriff Moody stepped forward, instead. With a grim expression she said, "I need to talk to someone from the Lambert family."

A brief hesitation, then B.J. stood, tall and lean in his charcoal suit and tie. "Savannah." His grim expression grew darker. "What happened?"

Olive made her way to her feet and said what everyone in the room was fearing. "Has there been an accident?"

The silence intensified as one second stretched into two.

"I'm sorry, Olive. But yes. There's been an a-accident." The sheriff's voice broke on the last word and Laurel could feel Winnie wobble on the delicate heels of her wedding shoes. On cue, Cassidy came up on the bride's other side and helped Laurel hold her steady.

Sheriff Moody looked from B.J. to the bride, then finally back to Olive. "Jackson's SUV hit a moose on Big Valley Road, about five miles from town."

The name of the road meant nothing to Laurel. She was holding her breath, praying again, not with sharp annoyance as she had at the airport, but with total desperation. *Please let them be okay. Just a few cuts and bruises,* she bargained, *maybe a broken leg or two.*

"Brock?" Winnie locked her gaze on the sheriff, who slowly shook her head.

"I'm so sorry, Winnie. Brock was sitting in the front passenger seat—the impact point with the moose. He didn't have a chance."

Winnie made a sound somewhere between a gasp and a cry, then pulled her hands free from the supportive hold of Laurel and Cassidy and covered her face.

Laurel wrapped her arms around her friend, her mind slipping away to the party they'd had, just last night. She and Corb had been dancing. They'd had a few beers. The lights were low and her body had tingled at the touch of his hands on her waist and shoulder. When she'd stumbled, Corb said, "Tired? Let me walk you home, sugar."

He'd done more than just walk her home. A lot more. Never in her life had she fallen for somebody this hard. This fast.

"What about Corb?" B.J.'s voice was stretched tighter than a barbed wire fence. "And Jackson?"

"Jackson was driving, wearing his seat belt and the air bag was able to cushion him from the worst of it. He's badly bruised and shaken, but he's okay."

And Corb?

*"Your other brother was in the backseat. He should have been fine, but I'm afraid he wasn't wearing his seat belt. As we speak he's being medevaced to Great Falls. I can't say how bad his injuries are. You'll have to talk to the doctors for that."

"Is he conscious?" Olive asked, her voice rough, eyes desperate.

The sheriff shook her head. "No."

Chapter One

Two Months Later

Laurel was making the rounds of the Cinnamon Stick Café with a fresh carafe of coffee, when she noticed Maddie Turner's mug needed refreshing. She paused to serve the stocky, gray-haired rancher, who glanced up from the papers she was reviewing to give her a smile.

"Thanks, Laurel. Could you get me another cinnamon bun, too, please?"

"You bet, Maddie." After two months of running the Cinnamon Stick while Winnie convalesced on her parents' farm, Laurel was a fixture with all the regulars. And Maddie Turner, owner of the Silver Creek Ranch, sure did love her baked goods.

When she'd first started working at the café, Laurel had drooled over the cinnamon buns, too. Now, just the sight of one of the frosted goodies made her queasy. Laurel tried not to inhale as she plated one of the buns, then passed it to Maddie.

Back behind the counter, she put on a fresh pot of coffee. As she filled the carafe with water from the tap, her gaze was drawn out the window to the line of willow trees that grew between the café and the creek for which the town was named.

Another lovely September day. She wished she had time to get out and enjoy the sunshine, but, as usual, she was being run off her feet.

When Winnie told her, ten months ago, that she'd fallen in love with a cowboy and was going to move to Coffee Creek to open her café, Laurel had thought *how quaint*.

Now she knew better. The café was charming to look at, the food was devilishly delicious, but the work? It was damned hard. The first month she'd had so much to learn, she'd been running all day long. Then, when she'd finally found her rhythm, she'd caught some sort of bug that she still hadn't managed to shake.

What she needed was rest, but she wouldn't complain. How could she, in the face of what Winnie was going through? Thank heavens for Eugenia, Vince and Dawn, Winnie's regular staff. Without their help, and willingness to work extra hours, she could never have kept Winnie's café afloat while her friend struggled to deal with the double whammy of losing her fiancé and dealing with what had turned out to be a difficult pregnancy.

Laurel still couldn't believe what had happened.

Imagine losing your fiancé on the day of your wedding. Actually being in the church, in your gown, waiting… Laurel felt sick every time she thought back to that day.

In the awful hours following the grim news, she'd canceled her flight back to New York, and she'd promised Winnie she would stay in Coffee Creek as long as she was needed, never guessing she'd still be here two months later.

But with Winnie laid up in bed on doctor's orders, what choice had she had? She couldn't let Winnie lose her business as well as the man she'd been planning to share her life with.

With a long sigh, Laurel replaced the coffee carafe in the machine. Maddie, finished with her paper and her coffee, waved as she made her way out of the café and into the ancient Ford truck angle-parked out in front. Laurel was clearing her table when Vince Butterfield, Winnie's baker, came out from the kitchen.

She couldn't believe it was eleven o'clock already. "Time to call it a day?"

He nodded, never one to use a word when a gesture would do.

"See you tomorrow, Vince."

He tipped his head in her direction, just half of a nod this time, then made his way out the back door.

Laurel still found it amazing that this man—a weathered and scarred ex-bronc rider who looked about ten years older than his real age of sixty-two—was responsible for the bakery's rich cinnamon buns, mouthwatering bumbleberry pies and buttery dinner rolls. He came in every morning, except Sunday, at four in the morning and worked his magic for seven hours before getting on his bike and riding out to his trailer ten miles from town.

Winnie had confided some details of his past to Laurel—a former rodeo cowboy with a drinking problem, he liked the early hours at the bakery since they left him too exhausted to stay up much past eight in the evening. Early to bed meant no late nights at the bar, which meant no more drinking.

"He figures this job saved his life," Winnie told her. Laurel wondered how Winnie knew so much about him. The man had never said more than three words in a row to her, and those had been, "nice meetin' ya."

The door chimed and Laurel glanced up to welcome her next customer. The smile forming on her face froze the minute she saw him.

Corb Lambert.

She'd heard he'd been out of the hospital for several weeks now. And had wondered when she was going to see him.

It seemed now was the moment.

He looked good, though his hair had been cropped and she could see a long scar on the side of his head. His dimple flashed when he gave her a smile, though not as deeply as before. Laurel figured he'd lost about fifteen pounds.

He came up to the counter hesitantly, holding his hat politely in hand.

Through the grapevine, Laurel had kept posted on Corb's recovery from the accident. He'd been in a coma for forty-eight hours, and in critical condition for several days beyond that. All in all he'd been in hospital for almost three weeks, with visits strictly restricted to family members only.

Or so Laurel had been told when she'd called the hospital to ask about him.

She'd wondered if maybe he would phone her when he was finally released, and when he hadn't, she'd told herself she shouldn't be surprised. He'd been through a lot physically, and had lost a brother besides. He wouldn't have time or inclination to think about the woman he'd flirted with, and charmed, during the week before his accident.

But now he was here, and clearly his smile and the sparkle in his eyes hadn't been damaged one bit by his accident. She took a cloth to the clean counter, willing her heart to return to its regular standing rate of sixty-five beats per minute.

"Hello, sugar. Looks like Coffee Creek got a whole lot sweeter since the last time I was in town."

She smiled, thinking he was feeding her the same line on purpose. But when she glanced up at him, she saw no recognition in his eyes. "Corb?"

He looked puzzled. Then he frowned. "Have we met before?"

Oh, Lord. She'd heard he had some memory problems after the accident. But she hadn't been prepared for this. "I'm Winnie's friend from New York City. Laurel Sheridan. I'm so glad you're feeling better. I was meaning to—" She stopped, wanting to say so much, yet not knowing how to begin.

He didn't remember her. How was that possible? He'd touched and kissed the most intimate parts of her. They'd stayed up talking until the wee hours of the morning, sharing their deepest secrets.

She'd told him her entire life story. She hadn't intended to—normally she was quite reserved—but he'd seemed so genuinely interested in everything about her.

The bells over the door chimed again, a fact Laurel barely registered until Jackson joined them at the counter and tapped Corb on the shoulder.

"You here to flirt? Or order coffee?" He nodded at Laurel. "Hey, Laurel. Any word on how Winnie is doing?"

"She's okay." Winnie had made her promise not to say a word about the baby. She wanted to wait until she was well enough to return to Coffee Creek and deliver the news to the Lambert family in person.

"Will she be coming back soon?"

"I doubt it. She's had some health issues, and for now it's good for her to be around her mom and dad." She glanced at Corb who was listening to the exchange intently, lines marring his high forehead and obscuring his charming grin.

"So you're Winnie's friend from New York? The one who was traveling down to be her maid of honor?"

"He doesn't remember much about that week," Jackson said by way of explanation.

Corb nodded. "Scared me at first. I guess I'm kind of glad I don't remember the crash." He swallowed. "But there's lots of other stuff that's gone, too. The specialist told me it's normal, though, so I'm trying not to worry about it."

Laurel knew she shouldn't take his loss of memory personally. But it was hard not to feel hurt that he didn't recall her at all. "Is it possible your memory will come back?"

He shrugged. "They say it could happen—but no guarantees." He stiffened his spine, and managed another smile as he offered her his hand. "Hard to believe I could forget a woman as beautiful as you. Must have been some knock to the head, huh?"

It was so weird to shake his hand, as if they were

strangers making their first acquaintance. Playing along though, she kept her tone light. "Nice to meet you—for the second time. I take it you're here for coffee. Like to add a couple of cinnamon buns to your order?"

"I'll take one, sugar. How about you, Jack—" He turned to confer with his foster brother, but Jackson was already on his way out the door.

"I'll skip the coffee for now and go put in that order at the feed store."

"I'll meet you there," Corb said. Then, leaning over the counter, he added, "Say, Laurel, I was wondering if you could give me Winnie's number at her folks' place. I've been meaning to call her and see how she's doing. My family's been treating me like an invalid. Mother put me in the guest room at the main house, and until today, wouldn't let me even touch the keys to my truck. So I haven't had much chance to check in on her."

"Sure." Laurel wrote the number on an order slip, then tore it off the pad and handed it to him. According to Winnie, none of the other Lamberts had been in touch since the funeral and Olive hadn't even returned the calls Winnie made to Coffee Creek Ranch. So Laurel was glad to see at least one member of the family willing to reach out to her friend.

"Maybe I should ask for your number, too." Corb's eyes glinted with charm as he folded the paper and slipped it into the pocket of his jeans.

Gosh, this was weird. He was flirting with her as if he'd never met her before.

"You'll find me here most of the time," she answered lightly. "How's your mother doing?"

The flirting light left Corb's face. "Not so well. She's

been spending too much time alone in her room. Now that I'm stronger, I'm trying to coax her out, get her working with the horses again. That's the only thing that'll cure her, I figure."

"I can't imagine your mother on a horse. She looks so fragile."

Corb laughed. "Looks are deceptive where my mother is concerned. But losing Brock has taken a toll. When Dad died, she didn't have the luxury of isolating herself with her grief. Us kids were a lot younger then and she had to run the ranch. Now she knows she can leave all that to me and Jackson—though to be honest, it's been mostly Jackson up until now."

When Corb fell silent, Laurel passed him his coffee and bun, and Corb put a ten-dollar bill on the counter, refusing change.

He lifted the lid off his coffee and was about to add sugar, when Laurel stopped him.

"I already did that. Two packages."

He gave her a puzzled smile, then headed out the door.

As soon as he was out on the street, Corb let his smile drop. The effort of being himself these days was almost more than he could bear. All his life he'd been the easygoing Lambert, the charming one, the peacemaker. Never had his family needed him to fill that role more than they did right now. And never had he felt less like doing it.

Corb looked at the coffee and the bun he was holding. He ought to gobble it down and head over to Ed's Feed Supply, where he knew Jackson was picking up that alfalfa mix for the new palomino his mother had bought three months ago.

She'd actually bought the horse for Cassidy, though she'd never admit it. As if a new horse—even a great horse—would lure his sister back to Coffee Creek.

No, like B.J., Cassidy had decided to make her own way in the world, which meant there were only two of them—himself and Jackson—to carry on. Work was piled up so high at the ranch, he felt like they'd never catch up. He had no right to be taking a break and yet he found himself settling on one of the pine benches that flanked the café entrance.

He took out the cinnamon bun, and with his first bite, he could hear Brock saying that he was marrying Winnie for her buns. He'd always give a wink when he said this, and Winnie would groan.

Corb followed the roll with a long swig of the sweetened black coffee. It had caught him off guard that Laurel knew how he liked his coffee. Why didn't he remember Winnie's maid of honor?

Leaning back, he allowed his eyes to close for a second. Though he wouldn't admit it, not to his doctors or his family, he was suffering from some terrible headaches these days. He figured they'd ease off with time. But in a way he didn't want them to. Brock had died and he felt that he needed to pay a price, since he'd been the one to live.

Well, there was Jackson, too, but he'd joined the family when Corb was already fifteen, so it wasn't like they'd grown up together the way he and Brock had. God, he couldn't believe his baby brother was really gone. That damned moose coming out of the brush at just the wrong moment had stolen so much from so many people.

He felt especially bad for Winnie. It was too bad she'd taken off and left the county. He wished his mother would call her, but at the best of times Olive had not been fond of the woman Brock had chosen for his bride and these were definitely not the best of times.

Thankfully Winnie's friend from New York had stuck around to help her out. That had been real good of her.

But even from this one meeting, he could tell that Laurel Sheridan was that sort of person. You could see the kindness in her eyes, a warmth that gave her pretty face a special glow.

He admired her hair, too. Thick, red and long, all piled up in a luxurious mess. He wondered what she looked like with it down. The fact that he'd probably already seen her that way but couldn't remember, made his head throb.

Stop it!

What the hell was he doing, anyway, fantasizing about Winnie's friend at a time like this? His family was in mourning, damn it. Besides, it was weird that he couldn't recall meeting her when she obviously remembered him.

Had they spent much time together in that week before the wedding?

He wished like hell that he could remember.

RIGHT AFTER CORB left the café, Dawn Dolan showed up to start her shift, her long, fine blond hair already pulled back in a ponytail. She came in the back way, grabbing an apron from one of the pegs on the wall by the freezer as she passed by.

"Busy day?" she asked. "I hope so. I could use some good tips. I saw this top that would look perfect with that new skirt I bought last week."

Online shopping was twenty-year-old Dawn's main form of recreation. Laurel wished she would spend as much time on her college correspondence courses as she did surfing the net, but that was Dawn's choice to make.

"Lunch hour rush is sure to start soon," Laurel said. "So that'll be your big chance to wow the customers and earn big bucks."

They both smiled at this—the café did well for such a small town. But big bucks? Hardly.

"Mind if I take a little break?" Laurel checked her hair in the mirror, pursed her lips and added some peach gloss. "It's been a long morning."

"No problem." Dawn glanced at the sandwich special Laurel had printed on the chalkboard. "Should I mix up the tuna salad?"

"That would be great."

Laurel dried her hands on her apron, then slipped the strap over her head and slung it on the peg with Winnie's name stenciled above it. She went out the back way and walked around to the front. As she'd hoped, she found Corb Lambert sitting on one of the benches.

Maybe slumped was a better word. His eyes were closed; he seemed to be soaking up a little of the noon sun, but his brow was furrowed. He looked like he was in pain. Physical or mental, she couldn't tell. She supposed he had a right to be feeling both.

She sat next to him.

Though he must have sensed her presence, he said nothing, and for a minute or so, neither did she. Instead she focused on the sun's glorious heat as it penetrated her tank top and jeans. It felt so good to rest. Why was she always so tired these days?

Across the street Laurel could see the post office and library. Though she'd only been in Coffee Creek for two months, Laurel knew the middle-aged people who worked inside each of those buildings. They were regulars at the café, too.

Tabitha, the librarian, always came to the Cinnamon Stick for her morning tea and muffin. Burt, from the post office, stopped in for his lunch. In fact, he'd be crossing the street for his sandwich and black coffee in about twenty minutes.

She turned to the man beside her. He'd opened his eyes and was now looking at her. "I'm sorry to disturb you," she said. "I just wanted to say how sorry I am about your brother."

There were many other things she'd wanted to say to Corb Lambert. But this was the most important.

"Thank you. And I'm sorry I don't seem to recall meeting you before. You're sure we did?"

"Oh, yeah."

He put a hand to his head, to the spot where his scar was barely visible under the stubble of his newly grown hair. "It doesn't seem real to me. The accident. Brock's death."

"Winnie's still in shock, too, I think."

"She and my brother were good together."

"Winnie was crazy about Brock."

"A lot of people were. Brock was a lot of fun, but a hard worker, too. My mother saw to that."

"She sounds like quite the woman, your mother."

He chuckled. "She comes across as delicate and soft-spoken. But once you get to know her you realize she has a way of controlling things from behind the scenes. Us kids used to knock ourselves out to please her. Some of us still do."

"I guess she had her hands full running a place like Coffee Creek Ranch. Must be a lot of work for her. For all of you."

"It is, but we love it. At least those of us who stayed on the ranch love it. My brother B.J. is more interested in the rodeo circuit. And Cassidy seems to be feeling the lure of the city. Mom is hoping she'll move back home when she finishes school, but Cassidy is equally determined to go her own way. I figure the two of them are too headstrong to live in the same county let alone the same house."

He put his hat back on and took the last sip of his coffee. Laurel thought he was about to leave, but then he started talking again.

"How about you, Laurel? How are you doing? I bet you never counted on spending this much time in Coffee Creek when you left the city."

"I sure didn't pack enough clothes for two months," she agreed with a smile. "Fortunately a friend of mine from work, Anna, sent me a package by bus."

"Are you missing the city? Coffee Creek is about as small as towns come, I guess."

"I grew up in a rural community, so it hasn't been hard to adapt."

"You did? Where?"

"The Highwood area. Our farm was five miles from Winnie's."

"Well, that explains how you know one another."

"We've been friends since our first day at school. Winnie helped me through some hard times back then. My mother died when I was eight. Then my father passed away the night of our high school graduation. Both times Winnie and her family were there for me."

"And now you're returning the favor."

"I wish it wasn't necessary. But yes. As long as Winnie needs me, I'll stay."

"I have to wonder. What drew you all the way to New York City in the first place?"

This was so surreal—she and Corb had had almost this exact same conversation during the drive from the Billings Airport to the ranch the first time they'd met. They'd had many follow-up discussions during the days that followed, to the point that she'd shared the most private details of her past.

And now here they were—back at square one.

"I was never all that happy living on a farm." Her relationship with her father probably played a big role in that. She and Corb had had a long conversation about this, too, but now she glossed over that part of her past. "Teachers told me I had a talent with words, so I studied English and after I graduated, I moved to New York and applied for every job even remotely related to publishing. Eventually I was hired by *On the Street Magazine* as a lowly online sales rep—but I was sure it would be just a matter of time before I was promoted."

"And were you?"

She smiled. "I was finally offered an editorial assistant job just a month before the wedding."

"I hope they're holding the job for you?"

Laurel hesitated. "They are. But to be honest, I'm getting some pressure to come back soon or give my notice."

Across the street, the door to the post office opened. Burt waved, then started in their direction. And then a rusted pickup truck rumbled in from the west, pulling up next to Corb's black Jeep Cherokee.

Laurel stood, and as she did so, felt the now-familiar queasiness in the pit of her stomach. "I'd better get back to work. Looks like the lunch rush is about to begin."

"See you, Laurel. It was nice talking with you."

They made direct eye contact then, and Laurel felt the zap of instant attraction that had first pulled her to him when they'd met at the airport.

But this time she felt a second zap, too.

The tiredness. The nausea.

It might not be a bug or the unaccustomed work at the café.

She could be...

No. She didn't dare even *think* the word. Because being *that* was the last thing she needed right now.

And she was pretty sure it would be the last thing Corb needed, too.

Chapter Two

At five o'clock, Laurel put out the Closed sign, then wiped down the kitchen counters.

The Cinnamon Stick was a small establishment, intended to serve primarily take-out coffee and baked goods, though Winnie always had homemade soup and sandwiches on the menu, as well. For those who opted to stay—and there seemed to be plenty of people who wanted to do this—there were four stools at the counter and two big booths on the window wall.

Laurel loved the colors Winnie had chosen for the bakery—delicious hues that made her think of pumpkin pie, caramels and mocha lattes. Unfortunately the idea of eating any of those foods was totally unappealing right now.

All afternoon the suspicion that she might be pregnant had grown into a near certainty. After all, she hadn't needed to buy tampons once since she'd left the city.

And she'd been too wrapped up in Winnie's problems to notice.

Hell.

Wasn't it her luck that just as things were starting

to work out for her careerwise, something would happen to set her back?

Not for the first time, she wished Winnie was here with her, which was silly, because if Winnie were able to stay in Coffee Creek and work at the café, then Laurel would be back in the city living in her cute, if miniscule apartment, working her butt off at her new job.

But even if she'd left for New York the day after the wedding, as originally scheduled, she'd still be pregnant.

Oh, Lord, she just *had* to talk to Winnie.

Once she was satisfied that the café was clean and ready for the next day, Laurel went down the hall. To the left was the customer restroom. To the right, a door that led to a staircase and the second floor of the building.

She was barely in the door of the one-bedroom apartment when the phone started ringing.

Laurel kicked off her sandals—oh, that felt good!— then dashed for the receiver, hoping it would be Winnie. "Hello?"

"Hey! How are you doing?"

Her friend sounded stronger. More like herself. "I'm fine. How about you?"

"I had a good day today. Really. Got out of bed. Showered."

Her tone was self-deprecating, but Laurel understood the effort that had been required. "That's good, Winnie."

"I gave myself a talking-to last night. Decided this baby was going to be a mental case if I didn't get a grip on myself."

"No one can blame you for grieving. It's only natural."

"It's not like I'm forgetting about Brock. That's not even possible. But I have to start facing a future that doesn't include him. Mom got me started on a knitting project. That probably sounds lame. It's really helping, though."

"Are you kidding? Knitting is cool." Laurel went to the sofa and settled in for a long chat.

"So how are things going at the Cinnamon Stick?"

"Pretty good." Laurel gave her the cash register totals for the past week, then filled her in on some of the day's highlights, omitting, for the moment, the visit from Corb and Jackson.

"That sounds great. I can't thank you enough for all you're doing for me."

"You'd do the same for me. You know you would."

"But you can't keep putting your life on hold. You have to book your plane ticket home. Tonight. I'm serious."

"And what about the Cinnamon Stick?"

Winnie sighed. "We'll just have to close it until after the baby is born. My doctor is saying work is out of the question for me. Maybe if I had a desk job. But I can't be on my feet all day long. It would be too much of a strain."

"I'll vouch for that."

"Oh, Laurel. It's exhausting you, isn't it?"

Yes. But for reasons she wasn't quite ready to explain. Not until she knew more about Winnie's plans.

"Are you going to stay with your parents until the baby is born?"

"It's looking that way."

"Well then, maybe you should rethink telling the Lamberts about the baby in person. Jackson and Corb were in town today and I felt awkward when they asked about you. They should be told. I mean, this kid is going to be their nephew."

"Yes. And Olive's grandchild. Believe me, *I know*." Winnie sucked in a long breath. "And I *would* tell them if I hadn't had such an awful relationship with Olive."

She'd complained about Olive before. And while Laurel agreed that Olive wasn't the warmest person, she did think Winnie was exaggerating.

"How can *anyone* not like you? I mean, you're so easygoing, without any strong opinions on *anything*."

"Exactly. I'm perfect, but Olive doesn't appreciate that."

They both laughed. Then Winnie continued, "According to Brock, my first faux pas was serving Maddie Turner at the café."

"Maddie's one of your best customers. Why wouldn't you serve her?"

"Because." She paused dramatically. "Maddie Turner and Olive Lambert are *sisters*."

Mentally Laurel compared the two women. "Impossible." Olive was fine-boned and elegant, while Maddie was sturdy and down-to-earth.

"Yes. *Estranged* sisters. I guess it's an unspoken rule in the Lambert family that no one is to talk to Maddie or even acknowledge the fact that she exists."

"How bizarre. What happened to cause the rift? Did Brock ever tell you?"

"He didn't even know. It's like some big family secret."

"And is that the whole reason Olive Lambert doesn't like you? Because you dared to serve coffee and baked goods to her sister?"

Winnie laughed. "Not hardly. Olive had someone else in mind for Brock. A daughter of one of her bigwig ranching buddies. It made her crazy that he picked me instead."

Laurel never knew whether to believe Winnie when she talked about Olive this way. "Is it really possible, in this day and age, that a mother would think she had the right to arrange a marriage for her son?"

"It sounds crazy. Yes. But you have to see her in action. She never raises her voice or argues—she has this passive-aggressive way of getting her way. Her children—in particular, her sons—can't seem to jump high enough trying to please her."

Laurel didn't doubt that Winnie believed what she was saying, but at the same time she suspected that Winnie's point of view was biased. Because Winnie also had a very strong personality. And it was possible that they had suffered from a clash of personalities.

But how unfortunate that they hadn't been able to move past their differences after Brock's death. The two women who had loved him most should have been able to share their grief.

"Have you considered selling the Cinnamon Stick and moving closer to your parents permanently?"

"I have," Winnie admitted. "Mom and Dad have been pushing me to do just that. But this morning I called the real estate agent who sold me the property.

Unfortunately, the market has softened in the past year. Even if I was lucky enough to sell the place, I'd never get back what I put into it."

Laurel took a moment to absorb this. "So you're stuck here?"

"Pretty much."

"Then you've got to make peace with the Lamberts. Living in Coffee Creek, you won't be able to avoid them. And think of what it could mean to your baby. He'd have all those uncles and an aunt and a grandmother...."

Another sigh from Winnie. "What you say makes sense. I *will* try to make nice with Olive. I promise. Just...not quite yet."

"Don't put it off too long, okay?"

"I won't. As long as you promise to get your butt back to New York and that fabulous new job of yours."

"About that." Laurel hesitated. Putting this in words was going to make it seem so real. But she had to face up to facts. And who better to trust than Winnie? "I'm not so sure that I *can* go back to New York just yet. I've come up against a bit of a speed bump."

"What are you talking about?"

"You know how I said I've been tired? Well, I've also been nauseous. And today I realized that I haven't had my period since I left New York."

Winnie's soft gasp was audible. "Really, Laurel?"

"Afraid so. I believe I'm about two months pregnant."

"So it must have happened right before you left New York. But I didn't think you were dating anyone seriously back there."

"I wasn't." Here was the tricky part. "Actually, it happened on the night of your rehearsal dinner."

"Shut up. It did not."

Laurel let her friend process for a few moments.

Sure enough, it didn't take Winnie long to come up with the right answer.

"That must mean Corb is the father? The two of you seemed awfully cozy that night, but I never guessed—"

"You were too busy being crazy in love with Brock to notice."

"Yes. I suppose I was." Pain registered briefly in Winnie's voice before she returned to the subject under discussion. "Have you told him?"

"I can't, Winnie. He doesn't remember anything."

"Are you serious?"

"It's called retrograde amnesia. Apparently he doesn't recall anything much from the week before the accident. When he came into the café today, he didn't know my name. He acted like we had never met!"

"How awful for you."

"It was bizarre. He started asking me questions—the same questions he asked when he was driving me home from the airport. At times I thought he had to be faking it, but he really doesn't remember me, Winnie. How can I tell him that he got me pregnant?"

"Back up a minute. Are you sure you're pregnant? Have you taken a test?"

"No. But—"

"You've got to take the test."

"I already checked the general store. They don't carry those pregnancy test kits. The next time I'm in Lewistown I'll—"

"No need to wait that long. I bought a couple boxes

when I took my own test. In case I screwed it up or something. Look under the bathroom sink."

Laurel suddenly felt shaky and weak. She realized she was scared silly. It was one thing to suspect you were pregnant.

Quite another to know for sure.

"Want me to call you back?" she asked Winnie.

"Are you kidding? I'll hold," answered her friend. "Now get in the bathroom and pee on that stick."

THE NEXT MORNING, Corb took a little longer with his chores than usual. Partly because of the nagging headache that he just couldn't shake. And partly because of a certain redhead that he wished he could remember.

On his way toward the ranch house, where breakfast would be waiting, he came across Jackson, carrying a sack of feed over his shoulder.

"Why don't you leave that for a bit and join Mom and me for breakfast?" Corb asked.

Before the accident, a typical day had seen him, Brock, Jackson and Olive eating together every morning after chores. But since Corb had been released from hospital, Jackson hadn't joined them once.

"Nah. I'd rather finish with the horses. I'll eat later."

Jackson was a quiet guy. Though lately he'd been more quiet than usual. Corb paused, wondering if he should insist that Jackson take a break and get some food.

But Jackson had already ducked into the far barn with the special feed they'd purchased for Lucy. They had another equestrian barn on the property for the American Quarter Horses which they bred for sale. The purebreds and the working horses were never allowed to mingle.

Then there was the cattle barn, clear on the other side of the yard, where Corb spent most of his time.

Coffee Creek Ranch was a big operation requiring lots of work—and while they hired several wranglers and part-time help in spring and fall, all the key positions stayed with the family.

With Brock gone, though, there was going to have to be some reshuffling of responsibilities.

Corb entered the main house from the back entrance, kicking off his boots in the mudroom, then washing his hands in the stainless-steel sink next to the coatrack.

Bonny Platter, their housekeeper for the past three years—a record tenure for the position—came to the doorway with her hands on her ample hips.

"I have pancakes and sausages waiting, but first you better get your mother out of bed. It's time she joined the land of the living."

Corb was damned hungry, having started the day three hours earlier on just a package of oatmeal and a cup of instant coffee. But he shared Bonny's concern about his mother.

"I'll round her up," he promised.

"What about Jackson?"

"Just spoke to him. He's giving breakfast a pass."

"Again?" Bonny sounded annoyed.

"Again. I'll go get Mother." Corb crossed through the kitchen to the hall that led to the master bedroom. After his father's death ten years ago his mother had redecorated the room with a bunch of flowery fabrics and pinkish colors. Now he always felt awkward when he was called to enter the feminine space.

For that reason, or perhaps out of habit, he hesitated at the door after knocking. When a full minute passed without any answer, though, he finally cracked the door open.

"Mom? Are you awake?" Ten o'clock on a weekday morning and she was still in bed. Prior to Brock's death, this behavior would have been unthinkable.

"Yes, Corb. Please shut the door. I'm not ready—"

He ignored her and strode inside, stopping abruptly in the near darkness. "Jeez, you can't even tell it's daylight in here. Why didn't Bonny open the curtains?"

He made his way toward the outline of the windows at the far wall, then pulled back on the fabric, allowing in the brilliant morning sunshine.

"Bonny didn't open the curtains because I asked her not to," his mother answered tartly. Normally she styled her hair in a sleek bob, but it was looking lank and gray today. An appointment at her hair salon was long overdue.

She squinted at him and frowned. "The sunshine gives me a headache."

Feeling the scar on his scalp throb, Corb could relate. But he didn't admit it. Instead he checked the tray on the table beside his mom's bed. The toast and coffee were untouched. "What's this? Mom, you have to eat. Come on, Bonny will serve you something fresh in the dining room."

Her expression turned contrite. "You're a sweet boy to worry about your mother, Corb. I'm just not hungry."

"At least sit at the table with me." He stood by her

bed, until finally she sighed and sat upright. He waited until she swung her feet to the ground, then held out his hands to her.

"You're kind and patient, Corb. Just like your father."

Being compared to his father was about the highest compliment his mother could give. It was curious, Corb thought, that while his father had treated all of them pretty much equally, his mother seemed to have a unique relationship with each of her children.

B.J., as the eldest, had always been the son that Olive expected the most from—until he'd decided to become a full-time rodeo cowboy. Now Olive rarely mentioned his name.

Brock had been the doted-upon youngest son, while Cassidy, the baby of the family and the only daughter, seemed to take the brunt of their mother's criticism.

He'd gotten off easy as the middle child, Corb expected. Often ignored, but that was okay with him. And if he suspected that his mother would have traded his life if she could have spared Brock's, that didn't bother him, either.

Frankly, he would have given his life for Brock's, as well.

He led his mother to the dining room, pulling out her chair and waiting for her to sit, before settling at his own spot at the gleaming oak table. Bonny emerged from the kitchen with two hot platters of food, pancakes and sausages for him, a boiled egg and toast for his mother.

Corb was reaching for a second helping of pancakes, when the house phone rang. A moment later, Bonny brought him the receiver. "It's Laurel Sheridan."

His heart flip-flopped at the mention of Winnie's

pretty friend. He reached for the phone, at the same time rising from his chair and heading for the patio door leading outside.

"Hi, Corb. I— This is going to sound strange but I was wondering if you could come by the café tonight after closing time?"

"That shouldn't be a problem. You close at five?"

"Yes. I— The thing is, I have something to tell you. Something that happened during the week before the wedding. I know you don't remember. But..."

Lord, but she sounded nervous. Was she worried he'd say no? But he was certainly keen to spend more time with her. And he was also anxious to fill in some of the missing blanks in his memory, as well.

He paced to the edge of the deck then stared beyond the outbuildings and pastures to the profile of Square Butte, the mountain that flanked the south side of their property.

In between were hundreds of acres of rolling hills covered with wild grass and dotted with patches of brush, aspen and ponderosa pine.

Usually the sight of the land—his family's legacy— filled Corb with a profound sense of calm and peace.

Today, he felt anything but peaceful.

There's something about this woman, he realized. Something he should be remembering.

"We'll talk at five," he promised, wondering what she had to tell him.

WHEN THE FACT of her pregnancy had been confirmed yesterday, Laurel had spent most of the night wondering how she would break the news to Corb.

She'd spent the better part of the day thinking about the very same problem. During a lull in business, around 9:00 a.m., she'd called the ranch to ask Corb to come into town.

He'd sounded surprised to hear from her.

Of course he was. In his mind they had only just met yesterday.

"My pie, Laurel?" Burt, the postmaster had finished his sandwich and was looking expectantly at the pie on display just twelve inches from his nose.

"I'm sorry, Burt. My mind is somewhere else today, I'm afraid." She lifted the glass cover off the stand and slipped a wedge of the juicy bumbleberry pie onto a plate, then grabbed a clean fork and set it down, too.

The door chimed and she snatched a quick look.

A couple of young mothers with strollers headed for the corner booth. Laurel smiled at them, then turned to the cash register so she could get the bill for the elderly couple who'd been waiting to pay for five minutes now.

Corb wasn't due for another four hours. She had to relax and focus on the present instead of fretting about what she was going to tell him. So what if she didn't have a plan? She'd just have to trust that she'd know the right words to say when the time came.

BY FIVE MINUTES to five Laurel was rethinking the wisdom of meeting Corb right after work. She should have given herself an hour to rest and get cleaned up. Every time she caught a glance of her reflection in the mirror by the sink, she thought she looked drawn and pale. Her feet and lower back ached. And she was tired. You'd think her body would have adjusted to being on her feet all day by now, but the job seemed to wear her out more and more each day.

If this was pregnancy, then it sucked.

And she still had seven more months to go....

And then she'd have a baby.

It was too much to think about. Better to focus on one day at a time.

The door opened, setting off a cheerful tinkle from the bells.

Expecting Corb, she was surprised to see a balding, middle-aged man looking hungry and cranky.

Right behind him was Corb.

Yesterday the cowboy had been wearing work clothes. Faded jeans and a shirt that had seen so many washes that the fabric was threadbare at the cuffs and collar.

Not today.

Today he was in dark, pressed jeans and the shirt he'd worn at the rehearsal party the night before the wedding day.

He came up to the counter, right next to the balding, cranky man and she waited to see what he would say. If it was anything about the town getting sweeter, she would know that she was stuck in an endless loop of *Groundhog Day*.

"Hey, Laurel. How's it going?"

"You remembered my name this time."

"No bumps to the head in the past twenty-four hours. Generally—and you'll have to take my word on this—I'm pretty good with names." He gave her a warm, approving look. "And faces."

Not five minutes had passed since he'd walked in the

door and already she was feeling it. Sizzle. For whatever reason this cowboy totally did it for her.

God help her.

"Excuse me," said the balding cranky man. "I don't remember your name, little lady, but I'm pretty sure I was here first. Doesn't that entitle me to some service?"

"Of course, sir. What would you like?"

"Two coffees and a half dozen of those sticky buns to go."

"Cream or sugar?" she asked, all too aware of Corb watching her.

"Nope. Black like the creek."

This seemed to be a standing joke in the town, since it had been named for the creek that ran through the town with water the same color as a weakly brewed pot of joe.

As she boxed up six of the cinnamon buns, Corb settled himself on a bar stool.

Laurel willed her hands to be steady as she poured the coffee. A few minutes later, she sent balding cranky man on his way, locking the door behind him and putting the Closed sign in the window.

Turning, she removed her apron and gave Corb a nervous smile. "I'll just clear off the dishes from the back booth, then we can sit down and talk."

Corb was off his seat in a flash. "Let me help."

They each carried some of the mugs, plates and cutlery to the dishwasher. When it was loaded, Laurel started a wash cycle, then stood awkwardly.

The kitchen seemed a lot smaller when Corb was sharing it with her. They stood so close that she could smell the scent of his soap.

"You must think it's pretty strange that I asked you to come here."

"Not strange," he insisted. "I was glad." He looked at her intently. "Since we met yesterday, I haven't been able to stop thinking about you."

His words gave her a warm, sweet thrill, and she was reminded of why she had fallen so hard for this cowboy, so fast. He was totally sexy and a terrible flirt. But he had a soft side, too. And could be disarmingly honest.

She poured them each a glass of water, then led the way to the back booth. She slid onto one bench and he settled in on the opposite side.

He looked at her expectantly.

Nervously, she sipped the water. "I see you're wearing your lucky shirt."

"I am." His eyes widened. "But how do you know that?"

Their eyes met and held. His, dark green and fringed with thick short lashes, were oh so familiar to her. But what did he see when he looked into *her* eyes? Did any of the memories of their time together come back to him?

Like their first dance, when he'd held her in his arms and told her he was glad he'd worn his lucky shirt because that night was turning out to be one of the best of his life?

"Laurel, ah, just how well did we get to know each other in that week before the wedding?"

Chapter Three

Despite the water, Laurel's mouth was suddenly too dry to form words. Here was her opening. But she still had no idea what to say.

Suddenly she wondered if it was even safe to tell him the truth. Weren't you supposed to be careful when dealing with people who'd suffered traumatic memory loss?

But the trauma was the accident—not their affair. No, she had to tell him the truth.

Absentmindedly Corb put a hand to his scar, then quickly withdrew it when he noticed Laurel watching.

"Is your head hurting?"

He nodded.

"Can I get you anything? I have over-the-counter painkillers."

"Took a couple of those before I came here. I'll be all right. The headaches aren't as bad as they used to be. I'm fine."

But he wasn't. Laurel could tell by the forced quality of his smile. It was just so weird to be talking to him like this—as if they'd truly just met. Could he really not remember kissing her? Looking into her eyes as they made love?

He shifted uncomfortably, and she realized she'd been staring at him. She turned away, pretending to check the view out the window. Anything to keep from staring at him.

Finally Corb asked, "Are there things about you and me that I ought to know?"

"Yes."

"Then fill me in, please. You can't know how strange it feels to have a whole chunk of your life gone totally missing."

"I hardly know where to start."

"How about when we met?"

"Okay. That's easy enough. It was at the airport. Winnie had an appointment so she sent you to pick me up."

"Really? Seems like I ought to remember that."

She smiled. "When you saw me you said it looked like Coffee Creek was about to get a whole lot sweeter."

He groaned. "Sorry. Usually I try to use that line only once per woman."

"We talked nonstop during the drive home from the airport. You took me straight to your ranch for a family dinner."

He shook his head, his eyes reflecting his inner torment at his inability to recall any of this. "Was I wearing this shirt that night? Is that why you knew about it?"

Laurel traced a pattern on the table with her fingernail. "Not that night, no. You wore it at the rehearsal party the night before the wedding." She raised her eyes to his, briefly. "When the music started, you asked me to dance. And when I said yes, you replied that it was a good thing that you'd worn your lucky shirt."

"So. We *danced* together?"

"Yes." *And a whole lot more.* But how on earth was she going to tell him? She could see that he was already blown away by just the few things she'd already shared.

"Wow. This is so freaky. It feels so unreal."

Yeah. Tell me about it. "Maybe one day you will remember. When the headaches stop, perhaps your memory will come back."

He gave her his charming smile. "I'd love to recall the feeling of you being in my arms. But I'm not so sure I want to remember the accident."

Pain resurfaced on his face, and Laurel could tell this wasn't the physical kind. Suddenly she went from feeling nervous to nauseous.

She put a hand on her stomach and took a deep breath. As much as she wished Corb remembered everything about their affair, she, too, was glad he had no recall of the accident. "The doctor told Winnie that Brock didn't suffer. That he probably didn't even register what was happening."

"Yeah. That is some comfort."

He didn't look comforted, though, and she realized that she wasn't going to tell him the rest today. He'd been through enough. Let him absorb the fact that they'd spent quite a lot of time together, first.

To be hit with the fact of her pregnancy right now just wouldn't be fair. Besides, maybe he'd remember their affair on his own if she gave him a chance.

"Thanks for filling in those blanks for me, Laurel."

"No problem. I thought you should know. But I

should probably finish closing up here and getting the place ready to open in the morning."

He took the hint with grace, getting up from the booth and heading for the door. She followed him outside, where the day was still warm and sunny. Once he was gone, she'd take a walk along the creek, see if fresh air would help her feel better.

"It was good to see you again, Laurel." Corb had been carrying his hat. Now he settled it on his head, preparing to leave, but for some reason, not heading for his Jeep.

Laurel couldn't answer. Since she'd stood up, her stomach had not been happy. Now it was threatening to heave the contents of her water glass all over the front sidewalk.

The feeling would pass. It always did. She put a hand on her stomach. Closed her eyes. *Please...*

But the feeling didn't go away. In fact, it grew worse. She needed a restroom. *Now.*

Cupping a hand over her mouth, she raced back inside, desperate to make it in time. Behind her, Corb called, "Are you okay?"

No. She sure wasn't.

CORB DIDN'T KNOW what to do. He couldn't just drive away without making sure Laurel was all right. Tentatively, he headed back inside the café and stuck his head down the short hallway that led to the restroom. He could hear retching on the other side of the closed door.

Jeez. That didn't sound good.

He waited for the noise to subside, then called out, "Can I get you anything?"

"I have everything I need here. Fresh water. Towels. A solid door between us so you can't see how embarrassed I am."

He grinned, glad that she wasn't so ill she had lost her sense of humor. There was the sound of flushing. Then her voice again, from behind the closed door. "You can go now. I'm fine."

"Hey now. No need to be embarrassed. If I worked in this place, I'd overdose on cinnamon buns, too."

"Ugh." Water splashed from the sink, a few seconds passed, then the door opened and a pale-faced Laurel stepped out. "Sorry about that."

His smile vanished as soon as he saw her. Despite her flippant commentary, she was obviously ill. "You look like hell. You'd better lie down."

"I will." She glanced pointedly at the door. "After I lock up behind you."

"I'm not sure you should be left alone."

"Believe me, I'm fine. I've had this bug for a few weeks now."

"That's a long time to have the flu. Have you seen a doctor?"

She gave him the oddest look. Then her face went superpale again. She put a hand to the wall, balancing herself.

He immediately sprang forward, placing his arm around her shoulders. "Maybe I should drive you to the clinic in Lewistown right now."

"No. No. That isn't necessary. I'll just head upstairs and lie down."

She didn't say anything more about shooing him out the door Corb noticed. So he stayed right behind her as she climbed the stairs that led to Winnie's apartment above the café. He could see right away that Laurel had been sleeping on the pullout couch in the sitting room. Sheets were folded on the chair beside the couch and a pillow with a white cover laid on top.

"I'll make up the bed for you."

Laurel didn't turn down his offer, just collapsed into a second chair, looking pretty much like death warmed over. What was wrong with her?

Quickly he removed the top cushions, pulled out the bed, then put on the sheets.

"You make a cute housemaid," Laurel commented.

She couldn't be *too* sick if she was still making wise-cracks.

"Yeah, but I don't do windows." He tossed the pillow on the bed, then pointed at her. "Lie down."

Obediently as Cassidy's old border collie, Laurel did as told, only pausing to kick off her sandals before sinking gratefully onto the bed.

"Good girl," he said. "I'll get you some water."

"Woof, woof."

He laughed, then gave her a quizzical look. Funny how she almost seemed to be able to read his mind at times. He went to the small galley kitchen and found a glass on the draining board which he filled with cold water from the tap.

"Anything else you want while I'm in here? Crackers or something?"

"Water is fine."

He handed her the glass then watched as she took a careful sip. Even though she was sick and pale, she still looked pretty. The freckles dusting her slender nose was just about the cutest thing he'd ever seen. He had an odd sensation of déjà vu, then realized he'd probably admired her freckles when they were dancing. Holding her in his arms, standing a good six inches taller than her, he would have had a perfect view of them.

"Was it a slow dance?" he asked.

She didn't meet his eyes. "Yes."

"I thought so."

Her lashes flew up as she looked at him. "You remember?"

"Just your freckles." He had the strangest urge to lean over the bed and kiss them. Once the freckles had been taken care of, he'd move to those rose-petal lips of hers. Why was it redheads always had the most kissable mouths?

Not that he'd dated so many redheads in his life. In fact—Laurel was pretty much the first.

This woman. She had a pretty strong effect on him. He'd better get out of here before he said or did something really stupid.

"If you're okay, I guess I'll be going."

"I'm fine," she assured him.

"Don't worry about locking up behind me. Coffee Creek is a safe sort of place."

"Really?" Laurel said softly. "Could have fooled me."

"I'M NOT GOING to be able to tell him, Winnie. I just can't."

Fifteen minutes after Corb left the apartment, when she was sure her stomach had settled enough that she wouldn't be sick again, Laurel had called her friend.

For the past two months all her focus had been on helping Winnie.

But now she was the one who needed help.

And, as usual, Winnie didn't let her down.

"Okay, let's say you don't tell him. What are your options?"

"I—I'm not sure."

"Well, how about this? Abortion."

Laurel's answer was instinctive. "No way."

"Fine then. Option two—you have the baby and give it up for adoption."

"No way." That answer had come out of nowhere, too, and Laurel was surprised at how sure she felt about it. She had been adopted by her parents, and she'd always wondered about her biological mother and father. Why had they given her up? She'd sworn that she would never do the same thing, no matter how dire her circumstances.

Well, these circumstances were pretty dire, but at least she was twenty-six, not sixteen as her own birth mother had been.

"Well, then. That leaves only one alternative. You're going to have a baby, Laurel. Just like me. We can be single mothers together. We'll be like a same-sex couple except for the sex part."

Reluctantly Laurel laughed. In some ways the picture Winnie was painting was almost appealing. But there was one big problem with it. "I'm not moving to Coffee Creek."

"Oh, I know. I was just teasing. But isn't it a good thing you got that job promotion? The extra money is bound to come in handy now."

In theory, yes. But she'd already tested her employer's patience with an extended leave of absence. What would her editor say when she told her she was going to have a baby?

"Oh, Lord, this is so complicated...."

"And you haven't even factored Corb into the equation yet," Winnie pointed out.

"But if I don't tell him..."

"If you're keeping the baby, you have to tell him. Can you really imagine any other way?"

Laurel realized Winnie had just talked her around in one big circle. They were back where they'd started, with no other option in sight.

Feeling as if she'd been saddled with a thirty-pound weight, she sank back into the pillows that Corb had plumped up for her.

"You're right. I have to tell him."

THE FIRST TIME Corb had driven past the location of the accident had been the day Jackson chauffeured him home from the hospital. A plain white marker had already been placed in the spot where Brock had died.

This was to be expected. In Montana, sites of traffic fatalities were identified in this way to remind drivers to take caution when behind the wheel.

What wasn't to be expected was the wreath of purple daisies that had been hung over the marker.

No one in the family had any idea who had put the flowers there.

Until now.

Corb pulled over to the side of the road, behind a familiar, rusted old truck. When he got out from the driver's seat and crossed over to the other side of his Jeep, he saw Maddie Turner. His mother's sister. The woman none of them were supposed to talk to.

His earliest recollection of the feud between the two sisters was when he was around six years old. His dad had been driving him home from his first day at school, and they'd stopped to get an ice cream from the freezer out front of the gas station.

A truck much like the one at the side of the road here, had been parked at the pumps. He remembered the woman looked old to him then, but he'd thought she had nice eyes.

For some reason, though, his father had ignored her.

This struck him as wrong. He was used to his dad smiling and chatting with all sorts of folk, whether he'd met them before, or not.

"Who was that lady, Dad?" he'd asked on the drive home, in between licks of his chocolate-covered ice cream.

"That woman is your mom's sister. Her name is Maddie Turner."

"Why— Then she's my aunt, isn't she, Dad?"

"Well, yes, but you shouldn't think of her that way. Long ago she and your mom had a big disagreement. That woman hurt your mom pretty bad."

His little-boy heart had been stricken by the very idea. "What did that lady do to her?"

"Your mom doesn't like to talk about it, and neither should you. Corb, next time you run into her, in town, or wherever, you just quietly go about with your business. Got that?"

"Got it, Dad."

Following family protocol, as established all those years ago, Corb supposed he ought to get back into his truck and drive away.

But screw family protocol. His dad had died a long time ago. Now Brock was dead, too. Why was this woman, who the family had disowned, setting out flowers for him?

Corb leaned against his truck to watch. The new wreath had been hung. Now Maddie Turner took the dead flowers and stuffed them into a black garbage bag. Then she started wading through the tall grass back toward her vehicle, without even glancing in his direction.

She was going to get into her truck and drive off without saying a word. And suddenly Corb knew he couldn't let that happen.

"Why?" he asked.

She stopped and stood still for a few moments.

She was about the same height as his mother, but built much stockier, carrying at least twenty-five extra pounds. Her gray hair was cropped bluntly at her chin, and her features were thick, her skin heavily lined.

She had none of Olive's delicate beauty.

Except for her eyes. Even at her age, which must be around sixty, he figured, they were large and a lovely shade of green.

"You are breaking the unwritten code, Corbett."

He couldn't say what shocked him more. Her speaking voice which was soft and refined. Or the fact that she not only knew who he was but used his full name, which almost no one but his mother ever did.

He decided to ignore the comment. "Why are you putting out flowers for Brock? Did you know him?"

"Just let it be, son." She blinked and a single tear rolled down the side of her face. Then she tossed the garbage bag in the back of her truck before driving away.

Corb watched, puzzled. Technically, Brock had been Maddie Turner's nephew. She had every reason to leave a tribute to him if she so desired.

But he couldn't help wondering if there was more to this than just that simple explanation. If perhaps Brock had broken the unwritten rule, too.

CORB GOT BACK into his Jeep and followed Maddie Turner farther along Big Valley Road, up to the point where the road forked. When she headed right, toward Silver Creek Ranch, the place where she and his mother had been born and raised, he turned left. He'd never been to the Turner place. Once it had been on par with his father's spread. But his mother had inherited a good chunk of the land with Grandpa Turner's death, and so now Coffee Creek was the much bigger property. Still, Silver Creek had to be a big operation for a single woman to handle on her own.

Corb was thinking about that as he continued on his way toward home. He knew that Maddie hired help, but no one lived out on the ranch with her, other than her animals. Word was, she had only her dogs and cats to keep her company.

Maybe the explanation for why she'd laid that wreath was simply that she'd gone a little squirrely in the head.

Corb drove past the entrance to the main ranch house, sticking left on the road to Cold Coffee Lake. Back in the days before Jackson came to live with them his father had commissioned three cabins to be built on the north shore of the small lake, one for each of his sons. The two-bedroom cabins weren't large, but they'd been built with plenty of space between them so they could easily be expanded, should any of them marry and decide to have children.

Corb had never thought to ask where his sister was supposed to live. He supposed his parents had the old-fashioned expectation that Cassidy would stay in the main house with her parents until she married, at which point she would move in with her husband.

He wondered if it had annoyed Cassidy that a cabin hadn't been built for her. If maybe that was the reason she was so determined not to move back to Coffee Creek after she graduated. He made a mental note to speak to her about the apparent inequity. There was more room along the lake for another cabin, after all.

Like his mother, he hoped his sister would eventually move back home. While he admired the drive that had led her to tackle the Accounting Master Program at Montana State, he wasn't sure she was on the right path. Cassidy had a way with animals that was almost spooky. Could she really be meant to spend her life working on computer reports and attending boardroom meetings?

Corb slowed his speed as he neared the cabins. The first one had been built for B.J., but as he was rarely home, he'd gladly relinquished it to Jackson years ago.

The next cabin was Brock's. Corb slowed to get a look at the porch, then sighed when he spotted Cassidy's dog, Sky, sleeping on the top stair, right in front of the door. With a heavy heart, Corb stopped the Jeep and got out. When Cassidy left home to go to college, her dog had moped like crazy for months.

Finally, she'd given her heart to another Lambert—Brock.

The two of them had become a team. Any time Brock was heading to the barn, Sky would be sure to be one step behind him. Nothing that dog loved more than keeping busy. But she was almost fourteen now, and most days she was content to lie in the sun and sleep.

Corb perched on the step next to the old dog. Slowly Sky raised herself to her feet and moved closer, dropping down again and settling her head on Corb's thigh. Corb obliged by giving her head a good scratch. Sky's beautiful black-and-white coat was showing more than a hint of gray.

"Poor old Sky. First Cassidy deserts you. Now Brock. But it isn't Brock's fault, you know. He'd be here with you, if he could."

Sky gave him a sad look. Corb knew she'd picked up on the names "Cassidy" and "Brock." But what he couldn't expect the dog to understand was that Cassidy would be coming back. While Brock never would.

Corb put a hand to the source of the pulsing pain in his head. How could he expect a dog to understand what he, himself, found so unbelievable.

Brock wouldn't be back. Ever.

He fought against the urge to lie down with the dog and give in to the grief. But that was Brock's mother's prerogative. The rest of them had to carry on.

He patted Sky's neck. "Change is hard, isn't it, girl? But you've got to stop doing this. My porch is just as comfy as Brock's, you know."

Sky tilted her head, as if considering the idea. Then she sighed, and sank back down onto Corb's thigh.

"Too tired to move?" Corb interpreted. "Let me give you a hand." He picked up the dog, thankful that due to the healthy food mix she'd been fed since her first day on Coffee Creek Ranch, and a lifetime of fresh air and exercise, Sky hadn't put on any excess weight in her old age and was still a trim thirty-five pounds.

Still, she was heavy enough, Corb thought, as he carried the dog and settled her in the passenger seat of the Jeep. Corb got back into the vehicle and drove the remaining distance to the third and final cabin: his.

He had work to do at the barns, but first he was going to grab a light meal and make sure Sky was comfortable in one of the chairs by the window overlooking the lake.

There was always work to be done on a ranch, but Corb liked being busy. While Brock had been in charge of the quarter horse breeding end of their operation, Corb was the cattleman.

As a teenager and young man, he'd worked under his father. After his father's death, however, when Corb was in his twenties, he'd taken charge of the entire one-thousand-head operation, with Jackson dividing his time between the horse and the cattle.

Corb wondered if his foster brother would be interested in working full-time with the horses now that Brock was gone. Someone would have to talk to him about that. He couldn't see his mom doing it, even though she was officially the one in charge. Still, he'd have to get her okay before he spoke to Jackson.

"Too much to do and not enough time," Corb told Sky as he settled the old dog on a blanket-covered chair that had been used for this same purpose every night since Corb was released from the hospital. He wondered how long it would take before Sky finally accepted this was her new home.

He hoped soon. It broke his heart every time he saw her waiting so faithfully on Brock's deserted porch.

Corb wiped away the tear that had managed to creep up in the corner of one eye, and went to the kitchen to fry bacon and cook up some eggs. As he worked, his thoughts drifted from the ranch back to town, and the pretty woman he'd left resting in the apartment above the Cinnamon Stick.

It had been news to him that they'd shared a dance at the rehearsal dinner. He strained to remember, but nothing from that day came back to him. Nothing at all. Laurel said he'd picked her up from the airport, as well. And he did have a vague remembrance of the drive to Billings. But he didn't remember meeting her, or chauffeuring her back to Coffee Creek.

It all defied belief.

How could he forget a woman like her? He found her fascinating to watch and loved her sense of humor. Something just felt right when he was with her.

And at just that moment, his phone rang. When he saw the number he smiled. This wasn't the first time they'd been on the same wavelength.

Chapter Four

"Um. Hi, Corb. It's Laurel."

She sounded nervous again. Maybe she was getting up her nerve to ask him out. Right. He should be so lucky.

"Feeling better?" With one hand he removed a package of bacon from the fridge, put the skillet on medium-high, then tore open the package and dumped the meat in to fry.

"Yes. No. I'm not sure. It's complicated."

"Well, actually, it's not *that* complicated. Have you gotten sick to your stomach since I left?"

"No."

"Are you still dizzy? Weak?"

"No…"

"Then you're feeling better," he pronounced, adding, "And I'm real glad you called to tell me. 'Cause I was worried about you."

"Y-you were?"

"Sure. Goes against the cowboy code to leave a woman when she's in distress."

"This cowboy code. Is that a real thing?"

She sounded so tense and serious. What had happened to that sassy sense of humor he liked so much? "Look, Laurel, let's cut to the chase. Are you calling to ask me out? 'Cause if you are, let me do the honors. Are you free for dinner tomorrow?"

"Oh. Well, yes, I am. But that wasn't why I was calling."

His head was fairly aching now, and he wished she'd get to the point. That anxious pitch to her voice was making him feel pretty edgy, too. He stepped back to the fridge to grab the eggs. "Would you just spit it out, already?"

He heard a long sigh from the other end.

"You know how I asked you to come to the café because I had something to tell you?"

"Yeah. And then I came to the café and you told me all the things I didn't remember. Like picking you up at the airport. And dancing together at the rehearsal party." He shut the fridge, egg carton in hand. "Wait a minute. You did tell me *everything,* right?"

But even as he asked the question, he suspected she hadn't.

"Actually, I left out some important bits."

"Such as…?"

"I thought this would be easier over the phone. It isn't, but here goes. Corb, I'm pregnant."

Corb swore his heart stopped cold in that second. At the same time, he lost his grip on the carton in his hands. It flew open as it fell, and all seven eggs splattered on the tile floor. Egg whites and yolks were everywhere, along with tiny bits of shattered eggshells.

"Hell!" he exclaimed.

"I'm sorry. I shouldn't have told you over the phone."

"I'm not yelling at you. It's the eggs."

"My eggs?"

"Not yours. Mine."

"But Corb, you provided the sperm, not the eggs."

He knew he should have seen it coming. A woman didn't call a man to tell him she was pregnant if she wasn't also calling to tell him he was the father. And yet, her words hit him like a splash of glacier-fed water to the face.

He stepped over the mess in the kitchen and collapsed in a kitchen chair. The bacon was burning on the stove. He didn't care.

He needed to catch his breath here. Gathering his wits would be a good idea, too.

"So, I guess we did more than just dance the night of the rehearsal dinner?"

"Yes."

He rubbed a hand over his face. "Why didn't you tell me earlier?"

"I don't know. Maybe I was afraid you wouldn't believe me."

He could hear the hurt in her voice. He only wished he could see her expression.

"This is way too complicated for the phone. I'm coming back to town so we can talk face-to-face."

As soon as Corb ended their call, Laurel phoned Winnie. "I just told him. I don't think it went very well."

Winnie made a sympathetic sound. "What did he say?"

"Hell. He said hell."

"Really? That doesn't sound like Corb."

"Now he's coming back to town so we can talk."

"Probably a good idea."

"I'm not so sure." Laurel's stomach was queasy again. She hadn't had time to adjust to the reality of being pregnant, herself. It had been too soon to tell Corb.

Thank you, Winnie.

But now the news was out, and she was going to have to deal with the aftershocks. She wished she had time to come up with a plan before she threw Corb into the mix. For sure, he'd have opinions—she was especially worried about that stupid cowboy code he'd mentioned.

"It was too soon to tell him. I should have waited a few weeks until I worked out how I want to handle things."

"And then you'd have spent the whole time being nervous about it. It's better this way," Winnie assured her.

"If that's true for me, then why not for you?"

"My situation is different," Winnie insisted. "For one thing, my doctor has ordered me to avoid stress."

Laurel couldn't argue with that point. Winnie's spotting had started the day of Brock's funeral. They'd both been terrified that she was going to lose the baby.

"Well, he's on his way here right now. What should I do to get ready?"

"I suggest you have a cup of peppermint licorice tea. It will help your tummy. And your nerves."

Tea? A shot of scotch whiskey would be nice. But that was off-limits to her now, she realized.

"I promise you one thing," Winnie added. "Corb is a good guy. He'll help you figure out how to handle this. The two of you are in this together."

Yes. Exactly what she was afraid of.

"I HOPE YOU don't mind that I brought you here." Corb laid a plaid wool blanket over one of the flat rocks on the bank of Coffee Creek. The day was still pleasantly warm, with about an hour and a half of sunshine left in it. "I think more clearly when I'm outdoors."

Laurel settled on one side of the blanket. "It's peaceful. I like it here, too."

On the drive to town his mind had spun like a bucking bull.

What did she expect from him? More importantly, what did he *want* her to expect from him?

He had no freaking idea. And that scared him more than anything.

From his backpack he pulled out the food and drinks he'd brought from home. Cans of sparkling lemonade, a few crackers and some cheese. A couple of apples.

"You're pretty good at throwing together a picnic on short notice." Laurel took out the clip that held her hair in place for work, and let the red curls float gracefully past her shoulders. Then she selected a cracker and took a nibble.

He sat next to her, stretching out his legs and planting his arms so he could lean back a little. He'd always liked this spot. Just a short walk out of town, with a screening of willow trees for privacy and a nice view of the creek. He'd never agreed with town lore that likened the water to cold coffee. To him, it looked like liquid topaz—all gold and gleaming in the sun. When he was younger, he used to bring his girlfriends to this spot to make out.

A sudden thought hit him. "It didn't happen here, did it?"

Laurel looked confused first, then she smiled. "Taken a lot of women here, have you?"

"Mostly when I was a lot younger. I can't remember the last time. But that's the point, isn't it? I don't remember being with you." And it was driving him crazy. He could hardly wait for her to fill in the blanks. "Please tell me how it happened."

"Well, as I've already explained, we hit it off from the moment you picked me up at the airport."

He nodded. He had no trouble believing *that*.

"We actually spent a lot more time together than I let on earlier. The first night you took me to Coffee Creek Ranch for dinner to meet your family and then you drove me home afterward."

"Why didn't you get a ride with Winnie?"

"She was spending the night at Brock's cabin."

"That makes sense. So...did you invite me in that night?" he guessed.

"It didn't happen quite that fast!" Laurel reached for an apple and took a bite. Then took her time before continuing the story. "The next day was the shower. It was a Jack and Jill event and you and I helped your mother decorate the house and prepare the food."

God, but it was hard to believe that so much had happened. And he remembered none of it. "And after the shower? Did we—?"

"No! I'm just setting the stage, Corb. Trying to explain that we actually did spend quite a lot of time together."

No wonder she was so hurt that he had no recollection of her. He met her gaze and held it for a few seconds. "I wish I could remember, Laurel. I really do."

Her expression softened. "A day later we had the rehearsal party, which was held at the town hall. Again, you and I helped with preparations, then later, after the dinner, there was dancing. I've told you about that part, too."

"I was wearing my lucky shirt."

She gave a wry smile. "Maybe that shirt of yours is a little *too* lucky."

He was surprised to feel his face grow warm. "So *that* was the night?"

"Yes. That was the night. You and I slipped out. It must have been around ten at night. You took me to your cabin and...well, we made love. It was about one in the morning when you drove me back to town. Winnie wasn't there yet, but I had a key and I let myself in. Then you drove back to the ranch and as soon as you arrived home, you called and we talked on the phone for about an hour before Brock finally brought Winnie back to the apartment and we had to say goodbye."

"Sounds like we did a lot of talking." He wondered what she'd told him, and what he'd told her. He felt so clueless sitting here beside a woman who knew so much more about him than he knew about her.

But more than facts, he wished he could remember his feelings. Had he been falling in love with this woman? Or had he simply taken the opportunity for a fun affair with a beautiful woman who was only in town for a week?

"We did," Laurel agreed. She'd finished her apple. Now she reached for more cheese. Corb was happy to let her munch away on the picnic. He was more interested in feasting his eyes on her. The days were still long in Montana in September and the air held that special clarity that came just before sunset. Her hair glowed like copper and even her fair skin took on a golden cast.

Oh, how he wished he could remember how it had felt to make love to her.

Laurel, about to pop a slice of cheddar into her mouth, paused. She blinked, then shifted her hazel eyes in his direction. For a long moment, the two of them simply gazed at one another. Then she put down the cheese and slid closer to his side of the blanket.

"You're giving me that look," she said, her voice low and sexy. It made him feel a little crazy.

"I am?"

"The same one you gave me that night."

He leaned closer. Irresistible. That's what she was. "And after I looked at you this way, did I do this next?" He put a hand to the back of her head, threaded his fingers through the silky, rich strands of copper, then lowered his lips to hers.

Sweetly, slowly, he savored the kiss. Then he withdrew a few inches to check her reaction.

"Yes, you did. And then, I did this." This time she reached for him, placing a hand on his shoulder, then angling her face as she leaned in for another kiss.

She parted her lips this time, and their kiss deepened, lengthened, sweetened, until time lost all meaning for Corb. He felt like he could kiss this woman forever, and never have enough of her.

But no kiss can last forever.

"So?" she asked.

He stared at her, his mind blank. Then he understood what was happening here. She'd let him kiss her—

encouraged him to kiss her—in hopes that he would remember what had been between them.

Part of him was angry at her for the ploy.

But, on another level, he supposed it had been worth a try. "Sorry to disappoint you. That was a great kiss, but I still don't remember. All I can say is it must have been a hell of a knock to my skull for me to forget something that wonderful."

She smiled at him sadly. "It's starting to look like you never will remember, isn't it?"

"The doctors did say that was likely." Then he asked her something he had wondered about on the drive over. "If you hadn't found out you were pregnant, were you going to return to New York without telling me about—us?"

She shrugged. "What point would there have been?"

"So…we hadn't made any promises or commitments?"

"It was only a week," she pointed out.

Only a week. "And yet long enough that you got pregnant."

Laurel gazed pensively at the creek burbling at their feet. "It doesn't seem fair, does it? That it would happen after just one time. I mean, what are the odds?"

Yeah, he'd been wondering that, too. "Didn't we use protection?"

She looked affronted. "Of course we did. Though you did mention at the time that you weren't sure how old the condoms were." A hint of humor brought out the gold flecks in her eyes. "On a bit of a dry spell, were you?"

"You could say that. A few months ago I split with

a girl I'd been seeing a long time. I haven't dated anyone since her."

"Jacqueline."

"Yes." When was he going to stop feeling this shock of surprise every time she revealed some new fragment of knowledge about him? "I guess I mentioned her?" God, but this was messed up.

"You said you were together for about five years. But that when Brock and Winnie announced their engagement, she started wondering when the two of you were going to get married."

He hadn't realized, until Jacqueline put him on the spot, that he wasn't ready to take that step. And when he couldn't even give her a date when he *might* be ready, she'd decided to end their relationship.

He'd been sad and out of sorts for a while. But not brokenhearted.

Which had been reassuring in a way. At least he'd known for sure that she wasn't the right one.

"So, back to the condoms," Laurel said. "Do you figure they were about six months old?"

"More than that. Jacqueline was on the pill and we were committed to one another, so we didn't bother with condoms. Those were pre-Jacqueline condoms."

Laurel's eyes went huge. "Are you saying that package was *five years* old?"

"More like six." He looked at her sheepishly. "God, I'm sorry, Laurel. I guess this is even more my fault than I thought."

She shook her head, then gracefully got to her feet and went to watch the water gurgling along in the creek. She tossed in a stone, then another and another.

"Try this." He passed her a stick and they watched it bob along in the water until it was out of sight.

"What about your love life?" he asked. "Is there anyone significant in New York?"

"I had been dating a couple of guys before I left for Montana. Neither relationship was serious. One of the guys is from work, so that's problematic. The other I met at the coffee shop where I always stop for my morning Americano. Nice enough, but as far as I could tell he didn't have a job and that kind of worried me."

Corb found he didn't like the idea of Laurel dating other men. Not even from a time when the two of them hadn't even met.

And then another thought hit him.

"Any chance one of those guys could be the father?"

LAUREL STARED AT Corb, unable to believe he would ask such a jerky question. If she thought there was a chance he wasn't the father, she wouldn't have told him that he was.

Besides, she'd just told him that those relationships were casual. He ought to know her a hell of a lot better tha—

Wait a minute. She kept making this same mistake, assuming that he knew her as well as she knew him.

He didn't. To him they were virtual strangers.

Still, it had been a pretty nasty accusation to make. Rather than lash out, she cloaked her anger in sarcasm. "Gosh. I never even thought about that. Silly me. Maybe Mitch or Ethan is the father of this baby."

Corb looked confused. Then sheepish.

"You can't blame me for asking."

"No? Watch me." It had taken them about fifteen minutes to walk from Winnie's place to this spot. Laurel figured she could make the return trip in half that time if she hurried.

"Hang on. We're not done talking about this." Corb started to gather their picnic supplies, then changed his mind and ran after her.

"Actually, I think we are. Having established the questionable paternity of this fetus, your work is done. Why don't you go home to your ranch and ride a horse or something."

"It's going to be dark soon. I can't ride a horse in the dark."

He tried to step in front of her to force her to stop, but she brushed past him. "You just said it's going to be dark soon and I don't know this area very well. Please let me pass as I'd like to get home while there's still enough light to see."

"Hell." He let his hands fall to his side and stepped out of her way. "I didn't mean to insult you, Laurel."

"Really? So that was supposed to be a compliment, I suppose?" She didn't know which was worse. That he thought she would be sleeping with three men at the same time. Or that she would tell him that he was the father of the baby when she wasn't sure.

Both were pretty bad, in her books.

"Surely you have to understand that it was a natural question. From my point of view."

"You know what? I'm not a fan of your point of view."

"Laurel…"

His voice sounded fainter. In another minute or two

he'd be out of hearing range completely. She was glad he was no longer following her. She had to get out of here before she either lost her cool…or dissolved in tears.

Chapter Five

Could it be true?

Corb stared up at the exposed beams of the ceiling in his loft bedroom. He had no curtains on the two-story-tall windows looking out at the lake and an almost-full moon cast so much light in his room he could see a cobweb dangling from one of the rafters.

The cobweb swayed with the airflow from the slowly moving ceiling fan. First one way. Then the other.

Just like his thoughts.

Was he really going to be a father?

The idea filled him with terror.

But also with hope.

In the wake of Brock's death, the world was a different place. When people you loved could be snatched away in the amount of time it took to draw in one breath, the birth of a new child seemed like a tremendously wonderful thing.

Despite questioning Laurel about other men she might have slept with, he didn't really doubt that he was the father. Her reaction alone had given him the answer he needed.

But at a high cost. He'd wounded her with his lack of trust.

Of course, it was a lot easier to trust someone if you could remember sleeping with them.

When dawn finally lightened the dark shadows in his room, Corb got up. He let Sky out for her morning constitutional, then grabbed a packet of organic dog food from the fridge and emptied it into her bowl on the porch. He freshened the water from the outside tap, then went round to the side of the cabin that bordered the lake.

A drenched Sky was just emerging from a short invigorating swim. In years gone by, she would be coming at him with a stick in her mouth, anxious to play.

But now she just walked slowly toward the cabin for her breakfast. Corb gave her a friendly pat as she passed by. Sky had frightened away the loons that often swam here at dawn, but the view was still beautiful, more so than usual now that the aspen were turning. He loved this time of year. Soon they would have to move the cattle in closer for the winter. This was a job that everyone in the family usually enjoyed. Even Cassidy and B.J. had been known to make special arrangements to take time off from their work and studies to participate.

It was the one time of the year, other than Thanksgiving and Christmas, when the entire family could be counted on to be together.

Only this year Brock wouldn't be among them.

As Corb went about his morning chores—Saturday was just like any other working day on a ranch—his melancholic mood lingered. He nodded to a few of the hands out working with the horses, but didn't stop to chat as usual.

There was only one man he wanted to talk to this morning.

He found Jackson in the office, checking something on the computer. His foster brother had been a part of the Lambert family since he was thirteen years old and had come up on charges of theft in juvenile court. Bob Lambert had been a good friend of Judge Danvers and he'd volunteered to take the kid in—father unknown, mother incarcerated on a drug-related robbery charge—as part of the state foster parent program.

Why Bob Lambert had decided to reach out to this one particular kid, no one knew.

Initially Olive had been resistant. Bob, who usually ceded to his wife's opinions in most matters, some-how prevailed, and Jackson had proven worthy of his benefactor's faith, never causing the family a lick of trouble since.

In fact, he'd soon become an invaluable contributor to the ranch thanks to his solid work ethic and an al-most eerie gift with numbers. By the time he was eigh-teen, he'd taken over most of the bookkeeping, fitting in the office work after long days working with the cattle and the horses.

Despite all he did around here, though, Olive never had, and probably never would, hand over control of the checkbook.

Corb paused at the doorway to the office. When they'd built the new barns six years ago, Jackson had taken on the office as his own project, designing a bank of oak filing cabinets, the desk and a floor-to-ceiling bookshelf himself. He'd done all the carpentry, staining and painting, as well, and the final result was worthy of a magazine spread in Corb's opinion.

Right now Jackson was sitting in the oak chair he'd purchased to go with the desk, staring vacantly at the computer screen with an expression of deep misery.

Corb had seen too much of that expression since his release from hospital. He slipped into the upholstered chair across from Jackson's. "So what's up with you? Why aren't you joining us for breakfast anymore?"

Jackson—whom Corb had heard described by the ladies as the "dark, handsome, brooding sort"—shrugged. "I'm not that hungry these days."

Corb flattened a hand over the papers Jackson was shuffling. "Look, I know it's hard. But we have to move on. You think Brock would want us to grieve forever?"

"Easy for you to say. You weren't driving."

He'd guessed this was about guilt, but hadn't wanted to be the first to bring it up.

"And what if I had been? I wouldn't have been able to avoid that moose any more than you could."

"Yeah, well, tell that to your mother. You know she blames me." Jackson stood abruptly, took a sheet of paper from the printer, filed it, then slammed the drawer closed. Then, as if the rare act of aggression had exhausted him, he bowed his head and closed his eyes.

Corb didn't bother to deny the claim. He had a vague recollection of sharp words spoken between Olive and Jackson while they'd been visiting him at the hospital. They'd assumed he was asleep, or unconscious, but he'd heard enough to know that what Jackson said was true.

"You have to forgive Olive. Brock was her favorite. She's hurting."

Jackson snorted. "You don't get it. I *don't* blame her. This is one time when I totally agree with her."

CORB HAD HOPED to discuss his dilemma with Jackson, but seeing his foster brother in such a miserable state, it didn't feel right to dump his problems on the guy, too.

So he went to the house, washed up and joined his mother for breakfast, once more trying to entice her to leave the house and get some fresh air. Maybe go for a ride on that pretty new palomino.

But Olive wasn't interested. She was staring out the dining room window, listlessly, when he left, and he shut the back screen door with more than a hint of frustration.

His family was falling apart and there didn't seem to be a damn thing he could do about it.

Except maybe solve his own problems. A plan was starting to take shape in his head, a vision of the future that included a little boy or a little girl. He was surprised at how easily the picture came into focus.

A baby he would carry in his arms.

Then a toddler, riding on his shoulders as he walked around the property.

He'd teach the kid to ride, to love the land, to care for the animals....

Corb drove one of the ranch ATVs back to his place. He resisted the urge to call Laurel, thinking it might be a good idea to let her cool off a bit more, before presenting her with his new idea.

Instead, he'd catch up on a few chores around here, so tomorrow would be free to spend with her.

He showered, then went looking for clean jeans and a T-shirt.

Nothing. When was the last time he'd done laundry?

He couldn't remember, and that had nothing to do with his injury and everything to do with his lax house-keeping skills.

Corb sorted through his piles of dirty clothes, trying to find something that wasn't too bad. His favorite blue T-shirt didn't have any stains. When he pulled it over his head he caught a whiff of a fragrance—sweet and subtle—that made him think of Laurel. Had he worn this when he'd spent time with her? He must have.

On his way to load the washer, he glanced at his unmade bed and tried to recall the last time he'd done the sheets.

Hmm. A long time.

He went back to strip the sheets, first pulling off the duvet, then tugging the bottom sheet from the box spring.

Out tumbled a pair of black undies. Much too tiny and silky to be his. Another tug and a matching bra was lying on the floor, too.

Well.

If he'd needed any more proof that he'd slept with Laurel—beyond the affronted expression she'd given him last night—here it was.

What to do?

Give them back to her, obviously. But should he wash them first?

He had a feeling the hot, regular cycle along with

the sheets would not be a good idea. Maybe gentle with cold water? It seemed a waste to do an entire load with only two tiny items of clothing, but that's what Corb decided to do. When the cycle ended, he set the wisps of silk and lace on a towel in the sun to dry.

God, he wished he could remember what Laurel looked like in these. Even more, what she looked like with them off.

SUNDAY. GLORIOUS SUNDAY.

It was almost noon and Laurel was only just out of bed. She took a sip of the decaf coffee that she had just made with Winnie's French press, then a bite from one of the day-old cinnamon buns left over from the café.

The food tasted great, for a change.

She was feeling much better than she had all week. She almost wanted to take another pregnancy test in case the other had been some sort of mistake.

Logically she knew this was crazy.

Probably her body was just enjoying the blissful pleasure of a day off work.

Sunday was the only day of the week that the Cinnamon Stick was closed and Laurel was looking forward to a quiet day of contemplation. Time alone to adjust to the reality of pregnancy. She put a hand on her flat stomach and tried to imagine what was going on in her uterus right now. Cells dividing and multiplying. Hmm. That was a bit of an oxymoron, wasn't it? How could they be dividing *and* multiplying at the same time?

Laurel lifted her mug for another sip, only to realize that she'd emptied the cup. The cinnamon bun was all gone, too. She was padding back to the kitchen for refills of both, when the doorbell rang.

There were two entrances to Winnie's upper-floor apartment. One was through the stairway that led to the café on the main floor. There was no buzzer on that door, just a simple door handle lock.

The other was via an exterior staircase that provided an alternate exit in case of fire. And it was this door that Laurel cautiously approached.

"Hello?" she called, without unlocking the dead bolt.

"Laurel? It's Corb."

Oh, hell. She was dressed in gray yoga pants and a baggy, striped T-shirt. Her hair was pulled up in a messy knot and she hadn't even brushed her teeth yet, let alone washed the sleep from her eyes.

Besides. She was still mad at him.

"Go away."

"I have something of yours."

And I have something of yours, she thought grouchily. *It's called a baby.*

"Laurel?"

Part of her was dying to open the door. The other part was still holding a grudge. "I'm thinking."

"I *do* have something for you. But it's really just an excuse to see you. I'm sorry about Friday. I'd like to apologize in person for being such a jerk."

That was better. She twisted the dead bolt, then opened the door about six inches. Corb was wearing jeans and a white T-shirt that showed off his upper-body build to perfection. In his hands he held a paper bag. She wondered if he really did have something in there. It looked pretty weightless to her.

"I'm listening."

"Good. Thanks. So, um, I apologize and I'm sorry for what I said about those other guys maybe being the father. You wouldn't have told me I was if you weren't sure."

She let the words soak in a minute. They felt good. "Apology accepted." She opened the door wide to let him in, and as she felt him take in her appearance, she held out a hand in warning. "No judging. This is Sunday, technically still morning if only by a few minutes, and you dropped by without notice."

"Actually, I was thinking you looked pretty good."

Oh, man, she loved this guy. Not just for the things he said, but for the honest way he looked when he said them. Like he meant them.

"So…what's in the bag?"

A grin teased up the corners of his mouth. "I washed my sheets yesterday and guess what I found?" He pulled out her missing bra and panties.

"Oh, my lord."

"If you don't mind trying them on, so I can verify that their yours…" He dangled the garments in front of her.

"Good try. But that line works better with glass slippers." She snatched them out of his hands, catching a whiff of fabric softener as she did so. "You washed them?"

"Gentle cycle. And I laid them on a towel to dry."

Adorable. This guy was something else. All the reasons she'd fallen for him came crashing in on her. She supposed she could excuse his jerky reaction to her news on Friday.

It must have been a hell of a shock.

"Well, thank you. That was nice."

"If I could ask a question?"

"Sure."

"Why weren't you wearing those when I drove you home?"

She could feel her face growing hot. "We tried to find them, but it was getting late. We agreed that I would come back the next night and...we'd look for them again."

"Damn." No mistaking the regret on his face now. "We sure had us some fun, didn't we?"

"Yes, we did."

"Do you think we could start over? You and me?"

"Start over in which way?"

"Like—go on a date together? Try to forget the past—well, I'd have an easier time with that than you would—but just enjoy one another's company. Simple as that."

She almost said no. But he was being so charming. And it couldn't hurt to try to establish a good relationship with the father of this baby inside of her. "I suppose we could try. What did you have in mind?"

"My favorite thing to do on a beautiful Sunday afternoon is go on a trail ride."

"I'm not very good with horses." She glanced away, and he immediately picked up on what she was thinking.

"You told me that before, right?"

She nodded. "But that's okay. We're starting over. I'll try to pretend I know as little about you as you know about me."

"And you'll come on the trail ride? My mom has

a pretty palomino named Lucky Lucy. A real gentle mount and she's in desperate need of a good workout."

"Give me fifteen minutes to get ready?"

"Take twenty if you need them. I'll wait outside in the Jeep."

THIRTY MINUTES LATER Laurel was in the barn at Coffee Creek Ranch helping Corb tack up two horses. Lucky Lucy, the palomino he'd told her about, was even lovelier than she had expected. She was calm, too, standing cooperatively as Corb put on first her saddle blanket, then the saddle.

"Want to attach the girth?" he asked.

"Sure." She moved slowly toward Lucky Lucy, introducing herself to the mare before gradually fastening and tightening the girth straps. As she got acquainted with her mount, Corb tacked up a sturdy quarter horse called Chickweed. He had a small pack he'd picked up from Bonny in the kitchen that he tied to the back of his saddle.

As they led their mounts outside, Laurel felt a flicker of anticipation for the afternoon ahead. It was true that she'd always been nervous of horses, but Lucky Lucy did seem very well mannered, and the day was so sunny and beautiful it was hard to resist, as well.

"What a gorgeous place this is."

Corb smiled proudly. "It's home. And I feel damn lucky to call it that. Let's keep the horses to a walk. You and Luce can get to know one another."

And maybe she and Corb could do the same, Laurel thought. She was determined to give this "fresh start" idea of his a fair shake.

After about fifteen minutes of riding single file, Corb brought his mount up alongside of hers. "So tell me," he said, "How is it you're nervous around horses? You sure look like you know what you're doing."

"Why thanks, cowboy." He looked pretty good himself. At one with his horse and his surroundings. She hadn't seen him this relaxed or at peace since the accident.

Surprisingly, Laurel could feel her own blood pressure dropping. She hadn't been on the back of a horse since she'd left home for college. Her memories of riding as a kid were pretty tense. Yet somehow she'd remembered the skills she'd learned back then, without any of the nervousness.

"Who taught you to ride?"

"My father." She could feel the muscles along her spine tighten as she said this. She glanced at Corb's face, the part not shaded by his cowboy hat, and saw, not the commiseration she'd expected, but simple curiosity.

Fresh start, she reminded herself. *Pretend you never talked about your family with him before.*

"My dad and I didn't have the best relationship. He wasn't mean or anything. Just sort of disinterested. When I was out riding with him, I was anxious not to make any mistakes."

Because, if she did, a weary look would come over his face, a look he would quickly mask as he patiently explained where she'd gone wrong and how to correct it.

He'd been that way no matter what he was teaching her to do, or helping her with, whether learning to ride a two-wheeler bike, driving a car, or filling out her college application form.

"What about your mom? Were you closer to her?"

Funny. That was exactly what he'd asked her the first time she'd told him about her dad. "Yes. Mom and I were close. But she died when I was eight. Want to hear the whole story or a condensed version?"

Two months ago, Corb had asked for the whole story. He did the same today.

"Okay. Stop me if you get bored."

He tilted his hat up so she could see his eyes. "Not going to happen."

Okay, then... "First thing you need to understand about my family is that my father was totally crazy about my mom. Nothing about my life makes sense unless you understand that."

"Let me guess. She had red hair and freckles, too?"

The compliment made her smile, but she went on as if he hadn't interrupted. "No. I was adopted. About two years after they were married my mother developed uterine cancer. They caught it early and she survived, but the surgery left her unable to have children."

"That must have been a lot to go through."

"Yes. Shortly after that my mom convinced my father that they should adopt a baby. I was only three months old when they brought me home."

"I bet you were a beautiful baby."

"Actually, I was kind of homely."

"Impossible."

The look he gave her made her spine tingle pleasantly. Suddenly she didn't mind telling her story for the second time. "I remember my early years being very happy. But then Mom's cancer came back. And this time she didn't make it."

Corb pulled up his mount. "Damn. That must have been so hard."

"It was. Especially since I was older and beginning to understand some things. Like why my father always seemed cool and aloof. It was especially noticeable because he loved Mom so much. Yet he was so different with me. What I figured out later was that he'd agreed to the adoption to make my mother happy. It wasn't something he'd wanted, at all."

"But surely—"

She held up a hand for him to pause. "I remember one day near the end. My mom was in bed—too weak to do much other than sleep. I overheard her ask my father to promise to take care of me. And love me."

"Which he, of course, said he would do."

"Sort of. He said he would take care of me for her sake. But he didn't say anything about the love part. Even though I was so young, I understood that he hadn't been willing to promise something he knew he couldn't deliver."

Chapter Six

Corb looked stunned, as if it was beyond his imagination that a father could not love his only daughter. But it *was* true, Laurel thought sadly.

"We should take a break," Corb said.

Only then did Laurel notice that they'd come upon the bank of a creek. She let Corb help her dismount and was surprised at how mushy her legs felt. "Gosh. I can hardly walk."

"Your muscles are in shock. Try moving around while I tie up the horses near the water."

Once he'd done that, Corb took off his hat and knelt by the creek to splash his face. The temperature was edging toward eighty already and Laurel decided to do the same, not realizing quite how unsteady her legs still were.

Corb caught her before she face-planted in the cold, mountain-fed stream.

"Thanks."

He gazed down at her face for a few seconds before releasing his hold. "Let's sit in the shade and keep talking."

They rested their backs against two tree trunks facing one another. Colt had pulled food and lemonade out of his pack and they opened their drinks and shared squares of chicken sandwiches.

"So what was life like once your mom was gone and you were alone with your dad?"

"Much different. Quiet. Lonely. I started spending more time at Winnie's. Her parents were kind enough not to complain even though they must have felt like they were raising two daughters, not just one."

"I'm beginning to understand why you feel so close to her."

She nodded. "I was lucky to have a friend like Winnie. We were at our high school graduation party the night I found out my dad died in a car crash. The police told me he'd fallen asleep behind the wheel and drove straight off the road into a tree."

"Jeez. What horrible luck to lose a second parent so tragically."

She hesitated. She'd told him more the first time they'd had this conversation, but maybe she'd been too candid then. "Yes, it was horrible. Once again Winnie and her family came to my rescue. I lived with them that summer while the lawyers arranged to sell my father's land and auction off the animals and equipment."

"That must have been overwhelming."

"Actually, between Winnie's parents and my dad's lawyer, I was pretty insulated. And I had college to look forward to. Winnie's father drove us to Great Falls and helped us move into residence. Winnie and I were roommates, so the adjustment to college life was pretty painless."

"So you left your hometown and never looked back?"

"I'd always dreamed of being a journalist and living in New York City. The farm was sold and even after the debts were paid off, I had enough money to go to college and study English. After that I moved to New York City, just the way I'd always wanted to."

"And you're happy there?"

"I have a cute studio apartment. And a really fun job. I do like it a lot." She hesitated before adding, "Winnie says it's time for me to go back. So I went online yesterday and booked a flight."

"You did?" He looked more than surprised. More like shocked.

"Yes. I'm leaving two Sundays from now."

CORB FOUGHT OFF the panic stampeding through his veins. He had to convince her to cancel that ticket. If Laurel went back to New York, he'd never see their baby. Never walk around the ranch with the munchkin on his shoulders, never teach the kid to ride or give him a chance to know his grandma and aunts and uncles.

No. He could not let this happen.

What was so great about New York anyway? So what if he'd never been there. He'd visited Billings plenty of times and could never get out of the place fast enough.

He had trouble picturing Laurel as a city girl. She looked perfect the way she was right now in faded jeans and riding boots, her hair wild and curly, and her face devoid of makeup.

Be calm, he told himself. *Take a deep breath. You can fix this.*

He waited for Laurel to finish her sandwich. "How are you feeling?"

"Like an eighty-year-old chimney sweep." Gingerly she got back to her feet, then immediately groaned.

"What about your stomach? Food staying down okay?"

"Thanks. Yes."

"So you're okay to head back?"

"Not sure. Maybe we should hail a cab."

"Smart-ass." He untied Lucy, then walked the mare over to where Laurel was standing. *Very smart ass, indeed,* he couldn't help thinking, as he helped her back into the saddle.

They rode back to the barn in under an hour and Laurel insisted on helping as he cleaned and put away the tack, then brushed down the horses.

By the time they were done it was almost six and Corb was starving.

And he still hadn't figured out what he was going to do to make her stay.

"Want to come back to my place for dinner? I have some steaks we could throw on the barbecue."

"Sure. I'll even make a salad if you have some greens on hand."

He opened the door to his Jeep for her, then drove the lakeshore road toward his cabin. As he passed by Brock's place, he was discouraged to see Sky on the porch again.

"Hell. That poor old dog just doesn't learn." He stopped, and was surprised when Laurel got out with him. She went to the old border collie, sitting on the stair and crouched low beside the dog.

"Hey, Sky."

He was startled that she knew the dog's name, then

realized since she'd been to dinner at the main house, she'd probably met the dog then.

Sky lifted her head, as if to return the greeting. Then she sighed.

"Poor thing. She looks heartsick."

"She used to be Cassidy's dog. Then she bonded with Brock. Ever since I moved out of the guest room at the house and back to my cabin, I've found her here every afternoon."

Laurel's response was to lay her cheek against Sky's soft fur. "Poor girl," she murmured.

"I'm trying to train her to accept that my place is her home now. But you know what they say about old dogs and new tricks."

"Hmm." Laurel patted the dog's head then looked deeply into the border collie's dark eyes. After several minutes of this silent communion, she glanced up at Corb. "Could we go inside?"

He glanced at the door to his brother's cabin. He hadn't been in there since before the accident. "Are you serious?"

She nodded. "I think that's what Sky wants."

It was the last thing Corb wanted to do. Seeing his brother's empty home was just about the most depressing sight he could imagine. But how could he say no?

He looked for the key hidden under an empty terracotta flowerpot, then used it to open the door.

Sky watched all this activity with eyes that were suddenly bright, and as soon as the door cracked open an inch, she was on her feet, nosing her way inside.

Corb gestured for Laurel to go next. He followed.

The smell hit him first. Never before had he noticed

that Brock's home had its own individual scent. But he noticed now. He took a few steps into the hall.

His mother had asked Bonny to have Brock's cabin cleaned and his clothing boxed and donated about a month after his death. Since then, no one had been near the place. There was a little dust, but not as much as Corb would have expected. His eyes skirted over the passport and travel documents lying in wait on the hall table for the honeymoon that would never happen.

Bonny must not have known what to do with them.

He swallowed, then stepped forward into the living area.

Sky seemed to be taking Laurel on a tour of the place. She'd started in the bedroom, then had gone to the bathroom. Now the dog and the woman brushed by Corb as they checked out the living room with its floor-to-ceiling windows and river-rock fireplace, then the attached eating area and kitchen.

The house was just like his. But in so many ways Brock had made it his own. Not the least was the vinyl record collection that filled an entire shelving unit made for the purpose. Brock insisted the sound was superior to CDs.

"Sky seems to be looking for something," Corb noticed. "Maybe a favorite old bone or chewing toy?"

Laurel came up beside him and smiled sadly. "I think she's looking for Brock."

He felt as if his heart had been squeezed, flattened and stomped on. Damn. Laurel was probably right, Corb realized, wondering why he hadn't thought to let Sky have a good sniff around the place. Dogs had their own way of collecting information and processing change.

And now that she'd been over every square inch of the cabin, Sky seemed satisfied.

She went to the door, and as soon as he opened it, made her way down the stairs, then along the path to his Jeep.

SKY WAS THE first one in the house when they arrived at Corb's cabin. She went straight through to the living room where she settled herself in her blanket-covered chair with the view of the lake.

"She's claimed the best seat in the house," Laurel said, amused.

"Never said she wasn't a smart dog." Corb showed Laurel around his home as if she'd never been there before. She made no objection, enjoying the chance for a second tour of the place.

It was absolutely charming. The floor plan was identical to his brother's, except for the furnishings and artwork. Laurel had been impressed on her first visit with the framed photographs on the walls. She knew he'd taken them all on the ranch, that photography was his hobby, and a pretty serious one at that.

But she admired the photographs as if she'd never seen them before. Loons on the lake at sunrise. A moose knee-deep in the water, nuzzling the calf standing beside her. A cow emerging from frost-covered branches in winter with a dusting of snow on her hide.

He had other pictures that captured the beauty in the little everyday things, as well.

In the bathroom was a series of wildflowers. In the hall, a photo of river rocks that stretched six feet across and only two feet tall.

"Can I get you a glass of wine or a bee—" He caught himself as he was asking her what she'd like to drink. "I guess the choice is soft drink or water, huh?"

She made her way back to the kitchen. "Yeah, I'll have to stop smoking, too, I guess."

At his startled look, she laughed. "Kidding." She opened the fridge and took out a lemonade. He popped the tab and poured it into a glass, with ice.

Then he touched her glass with his bottle of beer. "A toast?"

"To—?"

"A healthy baby?"

She nodded. She could definitely drink to that. And it did help to put their problems into perspective. If they managed to have a healthy baby, wasn't that the main thing? Surely everything else could be worked out with a little time and understanding.

Corb took one drink of his beer then set it down. "That was good, but I'd better go light the barbecue. Take a look in the fridge and see what you can find. I don't think I have salad fixings, but there should be some potatoes and carrots."

As she puttered in the kitchen, Laurel thought about Corb and the day they'd spent together. He was different. His brother's death and his own injury had changed him. He was no longer simply the charming, carefree, artistic cowboy who had swept her off her feet the very second she'd met him.

This Corb had layers of sadness around his heart. He weighed his words before speaking. And smiled a whole lot less often.

She knew his grief would eventually lessen. But he would always be a changed man.

Life did that to people. It knocked them around, sometimes to the point where there was no more telling what was up and what was down.

Twice she'd been there herself. After the death of her mother. And then her father.

Because, despite the fact that he had never loved her, she *had* loved her father. And his death had been a major loss.

She ate the steak that Corb grilled to perfection, and he complimented her on the veggies.

When the meal was over, they moved to the living room to watch the sun set into the lake. Or that was how it looked, anyway, as if the orange globe was slowly submerged into the calm, peaceful water.

What a life it would be. To live in a place like this. With a man like—

Corb was gazing pensively out the window. He could have any number of worries on his mind. But what Laurel saw was a strong man with a good heart. Two months ago, she'd thought she was falling in love with him, even though she'd only known him a week.

Now, she knew she had.

Just as she also knew that he didn't feel the same way. She—and her unborn baby—were just one more worry, one unneeded complication. What made it so much more maddening was remembering how different he'd been before.

When Corb had asked her if they'd made promises to one another, she hadn't answered, because it had hurt too much to know that he didn't remember holding her close and telling her there was no way he was letting her go back to New York. He'd never met anyone like her. *"I know you feel it, too, Laurel. This is a once-in-a-lifetime chance. Stay."*

Before she'd met Corb she would have laughed at anyone who said she would leave New York to go back to living on a ranch in Montana. But when he'd asked, she'd promised she would think about it.

She sighed.

The sound pulled Corb's thoughts back to the present. He got up from the sofa, full of apologies. "You must be tired."

She was. But he was looking at her intently, reminding her of that moment when he'd kissed her by the creek. And even though her muscles still ached, and she was weary, and ought to be asking to go home, all she wanted was for him to kiss her again.

Why did he have this pull on her?

He rested his hands lightly on her shoulders, then slid them up, along her neck, until he held her face gently between his palms.

His touch was like magic.

She wanted to fold into him, to feel his strength enclosing her tightly. And she ached to hear his voice whisper into her ear, saying all the words that had seemed to come so easily from him before.

Before his brother died.

Before he'd lost his memory.

Before she was pregnant.

Could lightning strike between them a second time?

She looked into his eyes, trying to mine their depths to find the answers she was searching for.

The green flecks sparkled, then slowly disappeared as he closed his eyes and touched his lips gently to hers. After a few seconds, he shifted his kiss to her cheek, and then to the lobe of her ear, where he said in a soft but heated voice, "You know what we should do?"

She nodded, imagining him taking her hand and leading her up the stairs to the loft, much like he'd done two months ago. She'd go more than willingly, remembering what a sweet and passionate lover this cowboy had been.

"We should get married," he said.

Chapter Seven

"This isn't—I mean you're not—" Corb's proposal had left Laurel breathless. "Are you serious?" she finally managed to blurt.

Corb looked hurt. "I'm not likely to joke around when I ask a woman to marry me."

"No. I'm sorry. I'm just surprised." In more ways than one. Surprised that he had asked her. And even more surprised at how her heart had leaped with joy when he did it. She'd always wondered at that expression, but it was true. When you were very, very happy your heart truly did feel physically lighter.

But that reaction faded all too quickly. Because she knew that duty and responsibility lay behind Corb's proposal. True, he'd said some lovely things about her, today and other times, as well.

But he wasn't in love with her. Not the way she was with him. And to say yes when there was such an imbalance in their emotions was surely a mistake.

But he might grow to love me....

It had happened before. So it could happen again. Couldn't it? She was the same person, after all.

But Corb wasn't. The accident had changed him. The question was, how much?

Corb took her hands. "Well?"

"Part of me wants to say yes," she admitted frankly. "But I'm scared."

"Me, too. It's a big step. And we haven't known each other very long. But I figure if we marry now we'll have some time for just the two of us before the baby comes."

He'd obviously thought this through, which gave her some comfort. And he seemed sincerely determined to make their relationship work.

The urge to say yes was growing stronger. Her feelings for Corb aside, the idea of having a baby on her own was frightening. She had no family in New York, or close friends like Winnie, the kind you could call in a pinch if you needed a sitter, or in the middle of the night if your baby was sick and you didn't know what to do.

But was she ready to leave New York? She loved her job. And she'd worked so hard for that promotion. If she gave up on her dream of being an editor for one of the big magazines now, she'd probably never have a second chance.

But she might never have a second chance with Corb, either.

"I think we both might be crazy. But I'm going to say yes."

She saw him swallow and wondered if the cause was nervousness. But the smile he gave her next looked genuine.

"You won't regret that decision," he promised her. Slowly he pulled on her hands until she was close enough to kiss.

And then he claimed her lips, the way he'd just claimed her future. She sank into the kiss, trusting him and loving him and ignoring the tiny warning voice in the back of her head and the pit of worry at the bottom of her stomach.

HE'D ONLY INTENDED a quick gentle kiss to seal their deal. But he hadn't counted on how sweetly Laurel would fit into his arms, or how absolutely hot her luscious lips would feel pressed next to his.

Her skin was the silkiest of magnets—he was drawn to touch every lovely inch.

"Laurel..." He looked at her in amazement, taking in her flushed cheeks, swollen lips, dewy eyes. She was incredibly beautiful.

They kissed again and he could feel her lovely, thick hair brushing against his face and neck as he delivered kisses to her petal-soft neck and collarbone.

Scatterings of freckles lay over her creamy skin, and the desire to see more—and *feel* more—was overwhelming.

Her quiet, responsive moan both inflamed him and brought him back to his senses. She was pregnant. And he'd never been with a pregnant woman before.

"Is it safe to go further? I don't suppose you've talked to a doctor?"

"I made an appointment for next week." She drew a ragged breath, then smiled with lips that quivered just a little. "I think it's probably fine."

He smoothed her hair back from her brow. During their make-out session her hair had seemed to develop a life of its own, growing thicker and wilder and framing her face so that she looked totally bewitching. His body responded with a deep, urgent ache that was part pain and part pleasure.

He satisfied himself with a gentle kiss to her cheek.

"Just to be sure, we should probably wait." He tucked another wild curl behind her ear. "But I have to say, that was a sensational kiss."

"I'd have to agree, cowboy."

He was relieved to see that they were on the same page with this. Marrying Laurel to secure his child's future was something he was prepared to do, no matter what. But it sure helped that his bride-to-be was beautiful and passionate.

It actually helped quite a lot.

CORB DROVE LAUREL to her doctor's appointment the next week. Laurel had been referred to Winnie's doctor, who had a practice in Lewistown.

She left the Cinnamon Stick in the capable hands of Eugenia Pyper, Winnie's oldest and most experienced employee. Eugenia was in her mid-fifties, a widow with a grown son who lived in Billings. She had a part-time catering business of her own and helped out in the kitchen as well as serving customers.

Laurel didn't tell Eugenia the reason for her doctor's appointment, but she suspected Eugenia had guessed.

"Must be something in the water around here...."

The comment made Laurel wonder if Eugenia also knew that Winnie was pregnant. She probably did. And since word hadn't spread around the town, that also meant that Eugenia knew how to keep her mouth shut.

She gave Eugenia a thankful smile. "Maybe the town should post a sign warning of the danger."

"All I can say is I'm glad those days are over for me, honey." She patted Laurel's hand. "Now get off to that appointment. Your man is out there in his truck waiting for you."

She and Corb had said nothing of their plans to marry yet, either. But obviously, where there was a baby there had to be a father, too, and Eugenia had everything all worked out.

Laurel checked her purse to make sure she had her insurance information, then hurried out to the truck.

Corb was standing by the open passenger door of his Jeep. He had on a dark green shirt with his jeans, and his left dimple was in full evidence as he gave her one of his most charming smiles.

As Laurel stepped on her toes to kiss him, she put a hand on his hard, muscular shoulder. "You didn't have to do this. I could have driven myself."

But she thought it was a good sign that he'd insisted. She liked the idea of marrying someone who was thoughtful. A streak of gallantry went a long way in smoothing out the bumps of any relationship, she figured.

The appointment itself was over quickly. The test was positive and she was given a prescription for vitamins and also an appointment for a follow-up in one month's time. The doctor assured them that sexual relations would not hurt the baby and then a nurse had them select dates for prenatal classes. Again Corb impressed her by agreeing right away that he would attend with her.

She'd thought some men—probably most—were squeamish about labor and delivery, but Corb sure wasn't.

"You better believe I want to be there when this baby is born," he said, placing his hand on her still-flat stomach.

Ten minutes later they walked out of the red brick building that housed the doctor's office together, blinking as the late-afternoon sunlight hit them.

The everyday world of downtown Lewistown looked so different to Laurel.

"Is this really happening?" She sank onto a wooden bench in the shade of a leafy tree. Corb settled next to her and meshed his fingers with hers.

"It's official," he said. "March 28, we're going to have a baby."

Laurel hesitated, wanting to admit something, but not sure if she dared. Finally she just said it. "I'm terrified, Corb."

"Me, too!"

Then they laughed, and went for ice cream, and Laurel was filled with a crazy optimism that maybe the two of them could actually get through this together.

On the drive home, Corb brought up the subject of their wedding.

"So what would you like to do? I know most girls dream of having a big wedding. But I was hoping you wouldn't mind if we kept it quiet and just invited immediate family?" He reached over the gearshift to grasp her hand. "Given that we're still grieving and all."

"I wouldn't want a big wedding anyway," she assured him. Maybe it was because she'd lost her mother so young and her father so tragically, but she'd never fantasized about a special wedding day the way Winnie had.

That didn't mean she hadn't yearned for love. She had. And did. She wanted to marry and have lots of children. Maybe even adopt a few, as well. A big, happy, noisy home was what she dreamed of. Not a fancy dress and a towering cake and a bunch of speeches.

"I can't even offer you a honeymoon," Corb admitted. "Fall is a busy time. In a couple of weeks we're going to start moving cattle in from the high country. It'll mean long days in the saddle."

Though she'd grown up on a small mixed farm, Laurel had had friends who'd lived on ranches and she understood what Corb was saying. The Lamberts owned a lot of land and a lot of cattle. Moving them closer to home for the winter wouldn't be easy.

"What if we combined our wedding and honeymoon into the same weekend? We could go to Vegas or Reno, just the two of us."

He looked intrigued by the idea. "You'd be happy with that?"

She nodded. "It would be good for us to have a few days to be alone together without the distractions of your ranch or Winnie's café."

"I like that idea a lot." He gave her a happy grin. "Now that everything's all decided and official, what do you say we swing by my mother's and give her the good news? She's already asked me to come by for dinner. This way we can make it a sort of welcome-to-the-family celebration."

"Oh." That was faster than Laurel had expected.

"Maybe you should call her and make sure she doesn't mind another person for dinner."

Corb laughed. "It won't be a problem. Bonny always cooks way too much food."

Laurel wasn't so sure. "At least drop me off at the apartment first? I'd like to change into a skirt and clean up a little."

"You look great just the way you are."

"Thanks for saying that, but I'd also like to follow you in Winnie's car so you don't need to give me a lift back to town when dinner is over."

She'd been feeling perfectly wonderful just minutes ago. But the mention of telling their news to his mother had made her stomach tighten and churn. Just in case she needed to make a fast escape, she thought it would be good to have her own car.

SCARCITY OF FOOD wasn't the issue when they pulled up to the ranch house thirty minutes later, Laurel a hundred yards behind Corb driving Winnie's RAV4 with Cinnamon Stick Bakery painted on both sides. Though Winnie had encouraged her to use the vehicle whenever she wanted, this was the first time Laurel had taken her up on the offer.

Not used to a standard gear shift, she had a little trouble at first, and she was sure Corb was laughing at her as she stalled in the middle of the first intersection leading out of town.

She'd changed into a dress and touched up her makeup, wanting to make a nice impression on the woman who would be her mother-in-law. As she drove, she thought about Winnie's contention that Olive didn't like her.

She sure hoped Olive didn't take exception to her, too.

The irony of the situation didn't escape Laurel. She'd come to this town expecting to witness Winnie's marriage into the Lambert family. Instead, she was the one who would become Olive's daughter-in-law.

She still couldn't quite believe it. Didn't think it would seem real until their vows had been spoken and the ring was on her finger.

By the time she reached the main ranch house, Laurel's stomach was very unhappy. Whether from nerves or the pregnancy, she had no idea. She waited until Corb had pulled up beside her before she got out of the car.

But just as she was gathering her courage to approach the front door, a third vehicle approached, pulling in behind Corb's Jeep. The woman driver, a blonde, took a moment to gather a few things before stepping out of her car.

Laurel turned to Corb, who had joined her outside the entrance to his family home. One look at his face and she realized he knew this person. And wasn't happy to see her.

The front door to the house opened then, and Olive, dressed and made up to her preaccident standard, appeared with a welcoming smile. She smiled at her son, but the instant her gaze shifted to Laurel all the warmth froze out of her face. She put a hand to her throat, as if under threat of attack. Then narrowed her eyes at Corb.

"What in the world is going on here, Corbett?"

Corbett? Was that his real name? That trivial bit of

information was pushed to the side as Laurel struggled to puzzle out the situation.

The blonde woman, close to her own age, Laurel guessed, was out of her car now. Her hair was sleekly styled and she wore a lacy black blouse with a short black skirt that showcased amazingly long, slender legs.

Yikes. Was this—

"Jacqueline." Olive's voice sure sounded warm now. "It's so good to see you again."

Her worst fears were confirmed. Corb's ex-girlfriend had been invited to dinner. Judging from the shock on his face, he'd had no idea. Clearly his mother had been doing a little matchmaking.

And Laurel's unexpected appearance put a very big wrench into her plans, which explained the chill Laurel felt every time Olive glanced in her direction.

But Olive didn't say a word. Ignoring Corb and Laurel as totally as if they were shrubs planted on either side of the large walnut door, she held out her hand to the newcomer, accepting a bottle of wine with admirable grace.

Frozen in place, Laurel turned to Corb for guidance. He gave her a smile, but she could tell it took some effort. Then he, too, greeted the blonde.

"Hey, Jacqueline. This is a surprise. Mom didn't tell me we were having guests."

"The invite was last-minute," Jacqueline explained. "Your mom happened to be out at the ranch talking to Dad about an upcoming auction this afternoon. I saw her and went out to see how she was doing, and we just started chatting...."

"I told Jacqueline that I missed having her around

the ranch and invited her to join us for dinner." Olive lifted her chin, speaking in a somewhat haughty tone. "I saw no need to inform you, Corb, given that this is my house and I'm the one who makes the arrangements for dinner."

The unspoken accusation was, of course, that Corb should have informed his mother about inviting Laurel. Olive was right on that point, and Laurel could do nothing but regret that she hadn't insisted Corb call before she agreed to come.

Her mistake. There were lots of families—and Winnie's was one of them—where a last-minute invite was no big deal. The Lambert family might have been that way usually, too. But not tonight.

Jacqueline hadn't been expecting another woman to be on the scene, either, and Laurel stiffened under her laser-sharp appraisal as they shook one another's hands.

"Come in, everyone," Olive said. "We'll have a glass of wine on the back patio before dinner. Bonny's left us a very nice baked salmon and spinach salad in the kitchen."

It would have to be a very nice salmon indeed, to turn this dinner party around, Laurel reflected. Corb's body language was awkward as he served drinks out on the cobblestone patio, at his mother's request.

Scattered around the patio, pots of mixed annuals were still blooming as recklessly as they had two months earlier in the summer at Winnie and Brock's shower. A table placed near the kidney-shaped pool had been set for three.

Laurel wanted nothing more than to turn and run.

Olive didn't want her here. Even Corb, she was certain, now regretted his invitation. And she couldn't help but wonder how he felt at seeing Jacqueline again. He'd never described the woman to her and she definitely hadn't expected his ex-girlfriend to be quite so beautiful. Except for the blond hair, she was a ringer for Katie Holmes.

And, clearly, she was Olive Lambert's choice for her son's future wife.

"So, Laurel, you must be planning to return to New York City soon?"

The question came five minutes into the meal, after Olive had adjusted the place settings and Corb had been sent to fetch a fourth chair for the table.

For all that the query was worded politely and asked in a mellifluous voice, Laurel understood the underlying meaning quite clearly. Basically Olive was telling her that it was *time* she left. That her presence at Coffee Creek Ranch was no longer welcome.

Across the table from her, Corb raised his eyebrows, a silent question asking if he should make their announcement now.

She gave a desperate, but tiny, shake of her head. She couldn't imagine a more awkward moment to tell Olive that she and Corb were planning to get married.

Other than that one question about returning to New York, which Laurel dodged, Olive didn't address any more of her comments toward her. Most of the dinner conversation centered around people Laurel had never met, events from the past she hadn't been involved in and plans for a future that she was not expected to be a part of.

When dessert—a blackberry cobbler—and tea were

finally served, Laurel looked forward to her imminent escape with relief. The salmon and salad had done nothing to settle her stomach and her refusal of wine either before or after dinner had earned her yet another disapproving frown from her hostess.

Olive chose that moment to address her second comment of the evening to Laurel. "What a shame that you don't care for your dessert. Jacqueline, I'm so glad you enjoyed yours. We had a bumper crop of blackberries this year."

"Oh, I'm a big fan of dessert," Jacqueline replied.

"Yet you're so slim." Olive seemed surprised and impressed. "You must have wonderful genes."

Laurel took a surreptitious look at her watch. When, oh when, would this dinner from hell finally end? One thing was for certain. She now had a lot more sympathy for Winnie. In fact, she could hardly wait to call her friend. They certainly had a lot to talk about.

CORB KNEW HIS mother had had good intentions when she invited Jacqueline to dinner. But he sure wished she'd given him a heads-up about it. Having Laurel and Jacqueline at the same dinner table was damned awkward. Now he was obliged to make polite chitchat with his ex-girlfriend, all the while dodging cutting glances from the woman he was planning to marry.

It was an exhausting balancing act for him.

And he was pretty sure Laurel was feeling pretty miserable, too.

So he wasn't surprised when, the moment she'd finished her last sip of tea, Laurel put down her cup and made a move to get up.

"I really should be running since we open the café at the crack of dawn."

"My chores come early, too," Jacqueline agreed, folding her napkin and placing it next to her empty plate.

"Oh, but you can stay a few more minutes, can't you? It looks like we're going to have a beautiful sunset. I'll make a second pot of tea and we can have a glass of brandy to go with it…."

Corb didn't think his mother realized that her invitation sounded like it was meant for Jacqueline, only. He got out of his chair and went over to Laurel, who was already up from the table.

"Stay?" he asked. Maybe once Jacqueline left, they would have a chance to deliver their news to his mother. But Laurel just shook her head.

"It was a lovely meal. Thank you so much Mrs. L—"

Suddenly her hand went to her mouth and her eyes widened. Having experienced this once before, Corb had a good idea what was happening next.

"This way." He took her elbow and led her to the patio doors. "First door to the left," he instructed as she raced ahead of him into the house. He intended to follow and make sure she was okay, but his mother stopped him with a question.

"I hope that wasn't what I think it was?"

Holy crap. Had she guessed so easily? He paused to scrutinize her expression, which seemed peeved and slightly scornful.

"I've heard this is how those city girls stay thin."

Corb was shocked when he realized what she was thinking. Shocked and a little angry, too. "Laurel isn't bulimic, Mom. She's pregnant."

As soon as the words were out, he wanted to yank them back in. But unfortunately a conversation with his mother wasn't like catch-and-release fishing. There was no stepping back, so he might as well keep blundering forward.

Taking advantage of Olive's and Jacqueline's stunned silence, he spilled out the rest of it.

"I'm the father and we're getting married."

Chapter Eight

"Laurel, you in there?"

It was Corb at the door. Finally. What had he been doing all this time? Laurel rinsed her face, then blotted it dry with a tissue rather than use one of the immaculate white towels hanging near the sink.

Seriously. White linen hand towels? On a ranch?

"Laurel? How are you?"

Poor guy was starting to sound quite worried.

"It's a good news, bad news scenario, Corb."

"What's the good news?"

"Whoever cleans the toilet bowls around here does a real nice job."

"That would be Bonny." He paused. "And the bad news?"

"I'm still pregnant." She released the lock on the door and let him open it.

He put his hands on her shoulders and studied her face like it was the periodic table and he was getting quizzed on it in ten minutes. "Is there any situation where you won't make a wisecrack?"

Then he didn't give her a chance to answer, just hugged her nice and tight. "You're so pale. I'm sorry you have to go through this. Guys really get off easy when it comes to making babies, don't they?"

"So far I'd say yes. And I have a feeling the hardest part is yet to come." Delivery. She hadn't even thought about that yet. And now wasn't a good time to start.

He laughed and eased back from her a little. "Now my turn for the good news/bad news routine."

"What do you mean?" She felt a lot better after that hug. Seriously, Corb should get a patent on his hugs, they were that awesome.

"Bad news first? When you got sick all of a sudden, Mom took it into her head that you had some kind of eating disorder."

Laurel had to think for a moment before she realized what he was saying. "She thought I was bulimic?"

"Yeah."

"That's crazy. People with bulimia sneak off to the washroom to empty their stomachs. They don't make a big scene and do the twenty-yard dash."

"Well, Mom's never actually known anyone with bulimia. She just reads about it in magazines and stuff. But of course I couldn't have her thinking that about you, so I—"

"Told her I wasn't feeling well," Laurel said hopefully.

"More like mentioned you were pregnant."

Oh, Lord. Laurel closed her eyes. Olive's impression of her had undoubtedly fallen another couple of notches after that announcement.

"On the plus side, we don't need to worry about breaking our news to her anymore."

Laurel's eyes flashed open. "What else did you tell her?"

"Pretty much everything. That I was the father. And that we were getting married." Corb's words flew out so fast she could hardly follow what he was saying.

When the meaning finally hit her, she was sorry it had. "Wow. Not exactly subtle, are you?"

He looked contrite. And he did a good job with it, she had to admit, managing to look so adorable it was difficult for her to be truly angry with him.

"That was a lot to hit her with at once. How did she react?"

"She fainted."

"Seriously? Your mother fainted?"

"Yup." Corb scratched the top of his head, as if the whole thing puzzled him more than he could say, then gave her another contrite smile. "I caught her before she hit the ground, so that was good."

"That *is* good," Laurel agreed, thinking of the stone patio. "Where is she now?"

"On the sofa. Resting."

"Oh my. And what did Jacqueline make of all this?"

"Well, I think she's given up on Mother's matchmaking plan, that's for sure."

Laurel put a hand to her mouth to stop a very odd inclination to giggle.

"As soon as Mother's eyes were fluttering open, Jacqueline took off. She's probably on her cell phone right now, telling everyone within forty miles of Coffee Creek about our news."

"Oh, dear. I need to call Winnie. And you should talk to Jackson and the others." She didn't want Winnie to hear about her plans to marry Corb via the grapevine. And he probably didn't want his siblings finding out their news that way, either.

She covered her face with her hands. "Oh, Lord. What a mess. Are we doing the right thing?"

"No doubt about it." Corb's voice was firm and assured. "Our family will be onside once they've had a chance to absorb everything. But I don't think now is a good time for us to talk to my mother."

Laurel was relieved. She didn't feel up to talking to Olive, either. "I agree. If you don't mind, I'd like to go home now."

"Sure you're okay to drive?" When she nodded he took her hand. "I'll walk you out to your car."

"Thank you." She could hardly wait to leave. Hopefully Corb was right and in time his mother would adjust to the news and become, if not warm, at least a little more cordial.

CORB SAW LAUREL off with some misgivings. He could tell she was weak and tired and he would have preferred to be the one driving. But she'd insisted on bringing her own vehicle and if he drove her back in that, then he'd be stuck in town with no way home.

So he waved her off, and stood in the driveway watching as the little white SUV—with the decal of a steaming cup of coffee in the back window—booted up the gravel drive on the way to the main road.

Not until the dust had settled did he head back into the house. He wasn't looking forward to talking to his mother. But it had to be done.

Olive was still on the sofa where he'd left her, sitting

now, and gazing pensively out at the land. He settled in a chair near the window, resting his arms on his thighs and leaning forward.

"Sorry for hitting you over the head with all that, Mom. We meant to tell you together. And gradually." He'd lost his cool when his mother had called Laurel bulimic. And Corb didn't lose control often, so he didn't have much experience in reining himself in.

"I still can't believe it." She shook her head slowly. "Can it really be true? Are you sure she's pregnant?"

He nodded. "I drove her to the doctor's office myself and was with her when they gave her the news."

"And you're the father?"

Corb hesitated. "Yes."

"But—how can this be? You hardly know this woman."

Corb was sure his mother would find it even more unbelievable if he confessed that he didn't remember sleeping with Laurel. Not that he was going to do such a thing. His mother knew he didn't remember the accident, but he hadn't told her that his memory loss extended to the week prior, as well. When it came to his mother, Corb had a habit of minimalizing problems.

But it was hard to make light of this one, and he could see why she was so doubtful. He'd felt the same, at first.

Still, he'd found Laurel's underwear in his bed, which made it pretty clear that they'd slept together at least.

Not that that constituted proof of paternity, but his gut told him that trusting Laurel was the right thing to do. Not the least because the alternative—losing out on a chance to be a part of his child's life—was just too much to risk.

Realizing his mother was going to need some convincing, however, he moved to the sofa and started the story as Laurel had relayed it to him.

"I fell for her as soon as I met her at the airport. With all the focus on Brock and Winnie in the week before the wedding, Laurel and I found plenty of time to…be together."

There. That was as blunt as he could put it. And by the frown marring his mother's forehead, he could tell she'd found it plenty blunt as it was.

"So, Laurel is about two months along?"

He nodded.

"Oh, Corb. And you're absolutely sure that you're…" She let the sentence trail delicately, as if even speaking the words was too much for her.

He nodded again.

"But you will insist on DNA testing when the baby is born?"

"Mom, no. I'm not going to ask that of Laurel, and you sure as hell better not suggest anything like that to her, either."

His mother had been stronger the past few days and it was time he set her straight on this. "I won't have Laurel insulted like that."

The words had needed to be said, but he couldn't help wondering if he'd been too harsh when he noticed tears glimmering in his mother's eyes.

"Son, I so wish your father was here right now to give you advice. But I have to ask. Are you certain that marriage is…the right solution?"

"What other solution is there?"

"I'm not suggesting you shirk your duty. There are such things as child support payments."

Corb couldn't believe she was saying this. He'd been certain that once she understood the situation his mother would stand by his decision. That she, like him, would believe it was the honorable course of action to take.

"I just worry about the long-term feasibility of your marriage. Of all my children, you're the one who feels the strongest connection to the land. You could only be happy here, on Coffee Creek Ranch."

He wouldn't argue that point. "And this is where we plan to live. At the cabin. At some point we'll add on an extra bedroom or two...." Something he hadn't had time to discuss with Laurel yet. But he would.

"Are you sure she'll be happy? She may have grown up on a farm, but she's a city girl now, Corb. And not just any city, but New York. After a while, aren't you afraid she'll get bored of our simple way of life?"

"We don't get bored. Why should she?" But Corb knew his mother had a point and it was one that he'd already found vaguely troubling.

"You and I love the cattle ranching business," his mother said gently. "And Jacqueline does, too, which is why I invited her to dinner, as I'm sure you've guessed."

"Mom—"

She put up a hand to stop his objection. "B.J. and Cassidy both moved away because they wanted more. And they're family. Don't you think it's likely that eventually Laurel will feel the same way?"

He wanted to argue. But he had no facts to counter with. So, miserably he sat there and let his mother continue.

"You've only known her a few months—and most of that time you were in bed recovering from the accident. How can you possibly know her well enough to take this big step?"

"I do know her. Look how she's stuck by Winnie since the accident. Not many people would drop everything to help a friend in trouble. She's a good person and besides—"

He moved over to the sofa, putting a hand on his mother's shoulder and looking her square in the eyes. "You said you wished Dad were here to give me his advice. Well, I don't need to hear him say the words to know what he would tell me. Family comes first. I must have heard him say those words a hundred times."

"That's true."

"Laurel's unborn child is going to be a Lambert, Mom. One of us. If I have to marry her to keep her and the baby here in Coffee Creek, that's exactly what I'm going to do."

CORB MADE HIS mother a cup of tea before he left her for the night. It was almost dark now and the amber glow from the sunset was reflecting in his rearview mirror as he drove from the main house down the graveled lake road.

He was pretty sure he'd convinced his mother that he was taking the right course here.

But he wished he could understand why he didn't feel more at peace about it himself.

Clearly he and Laurel had the sexual attraction thing

happening. He couldn't look at her without wanting her. And she must feel the same way, or she wouldn't have spent that night with him.

Besides, he liked her. Really liked her. She was fun to be with, interesting. And a good person.

His mother's well-intentioned concerns notwithstanding, he thought they had a damn good shot at making their marriage work.

So why the knot in the pit of his stomach?

He didn't think it was Brock's death or his lost week of memories that was plaguing him. No, this feeling was more like the awful churning in his gut that he would get when he was a boy and knew he'd done something wrong.

But he hadn't done wrong here.

Oh, making that mistake with condoms had been wrong. But he'd taken responsibility for that.

As he approached Brock's place, Corb eased off the accelerator and craned his neck for a look at the porch. No Sky. Interesting. He continued to his own place, where he found the border collie lounging on his porch.

So Laurel had been right. All Sky had wanted was the chance to check out Brock's place. Whether to make sure he was truly gone, or as a final gesture of farewell, Corb couldn't be sure.

He guessed Sky, so smart, and so tuned in to the feelings of this family, was capable of both.

"Good girl, Sky. You know where home is now, don't you, girl?"

She scrambled to her feet, gave him a good sniff, then looked hopefully at the empty food bowl next to the door.

"I'll get right on that," he promised her as he let himself inside.

He was glad that Sky was no longer keeping vigil at Brock's cabin, but it made him kind of sad, too. Life was going on, and while that was only natural, it still kind of hurt to see it happen.

"WINNIE? I HOPE I'm not calling too late?" Laurel was cuddled under the covers of the pullout couch, a cup of peppermint licorice tea beside her. Even though her friend had offered the use of her bedroom, Laurel hadn't made the transition. Moving into the bedroom would have seemed too permanent. Besides, she'd been hoping that Winnie would get the all-clear from her doctor soon and come home.

But that wasn't likely to happen for a long time.

"It's only nine," Winnie scoffed. "Of course it isn't too late. Am I ever glad you've called. At first it was nice having Mom fuss over me. But I've caught up on all my favorite shows, my eyes are strained from reading and I've got calluses from knitting too much...."

For Laurel, who'd lost her own mother so young, getting fussed over didn't sound like something she could ever tire of. Especially not with a mother like Adele, who knew how to be caring and supportive without crossing the line into meddlesome and manipulative.

Now, if Olive was her mother, that would be a different question....

"There have been no dull moments here, trust me."

"Did you book your flight back to New York?"

"I did. And I just canceled it."

"Why?" Winnie asked, her voice animated with curiosity.

Laurel took a deep breath. "Because I'm staying in Coffee Creek. Corb asked me to marry him."

"Wow."

"Yeah. It is kind of a wow thing, isn't it?"

Winnie's reaction was reassuring. "Oh, I'm glad! It's going to be great to have you in Coffee Creek. Our kids are going to grow up to be best friends, just like we are."

Those were things Laurel wanted, too. So very much.

"I'd love to live close to you again, Winnie. But—it's weird, isn't it? I mean, *you* were the one who was supposed to be living on Coffee Creek Ranch. Not to mention have Olive Lambert for your mother-in-law."

Winnie laughed. "I'm guessing you've seen her other side by now? The one she only shows prospective daughters-in-law that she doesn't approve of?"

"She invited Corb's ex-girlfriend to dinner tonight. Totally fawned all over her. And froze me out."

Winnie groaned sympathetically. "Sounds like Olive. Did Corb notice?"

"Not really."

"Brock, either. Those boys have a real blind side when it comes to their mother."

Laurel agreed, uneasily. Marrying Corb meant signing up for a lifetime with Olive, too. Now that was something grim to think about.

"Have you told your boss at the magazine that you won't be coming back?"

"Not yet. Corb just proposed. It's going to take a bit of time for all of this to feel real."

"It must be hard when you just got that promotion, huh? I know how much that job meant to you."

"It really was a great job. But getting pregnant was going to change everything, even if I hadn't accepted Corb's proposal. First there'd be maternity leave and then the problem of finding child care when I was ready to return to work."

"Having a baby makes life a whole lot more complicated," Winnie agreed. "I hate being away from the Cinnamon Stick, but I won't come back until I know it's the right thing for me and my baby."

"I'm glad, Winnie. You have your priorities straight."

"At the same time, I don't want you to feel locked into managing the café for me while I'm gone. Anytime you want to shut it up and go live with Corb on the ranch, please do so."

"Thanks, Winnie. I must admit there are times when I wish I had more freedom. But I can't imagine not having a job of any kind. Plus I worry about the staff. Eugenia has her catering, at least. But Dawn has an internet shopping habit to support."

Winnie laughed.

"And what about Vince. Didn't you tell me that this job has helped him stay sober?"

"It's true. Maybe one solution would be to hire another staff member, so you wouldn't have to continue to work so hard."

"I'll have a staff meeting and we'll talk about it," Laurel promised. "As long as you follow doctor's orders, and take care of yourself."

"Will do." Then, just before they said goodbye for the evening, Winnie added one last comment. "And Laurel?

Congratulations on your engagement. I always thought Corb would be perfect for you. It wasn't a coincidence that I asked him to pick you up at the airport."

THE NEXT MORNING at ten o'clock, Laurel was presented with the perfect opportunity for an impromptu staff meeting. Vince was nearing the end of his shift and Eugenia had just shown up for hers, when Dawn came in to see if she could get an advance from her next paycheck.

Business was at a lull, so Laurel made the decision to flip over the Closed sign and lock the door for fifteen minutes.

"Look, guys," she said without preamble. "We have some decisions to make. Winnie's health is still an issue. She won't be coming back in the foreseeable future."

Dawn stopped chewing her gum—a habit she never indulged in when she was working, thank goodness—and looked worried. "Is she okay?"

"She will be." Laurel avoided looking at Eugenia, hoping the older woman wouldn't share her suspicions about Winnie being pregnant. It wouldn't be right for the staff at the Cinnamon Stick to hear about Winnie and Brock's baby before the Lambert family did.

Fortunately, Eugenia didn't say a word.

"Which leaves us with the problem of how to keep the café running during her absence. Unless you all just want to close shop until she returns?"

"Not an option." Vince looked grim. "I'll work a twelve-hour day, six days a week, if need be."

Laurel had never heard him say so much at one time. Which only went to show how much this job did mean to him.

"I'm sure Winnie would appreciate that, Vince. But that shouldn't be necessary. We could always hire a fourth staff member. Or…divvy up the extra hours between all four of us."

"*I'd* love some extra hours," Dawn said.

Eugenia was less enthusiastic. "I could handle a *few* more."

"Put me down for two extra hours every day," Vince said. "I can take care of some of the supply ordering and bill paying."

"Awesome. You guys are the greatest." Laurel got out the calendar and without much fuss, they were able to come up with a working schedule that would keep the café open and suit everyone's needs.

Once she'd finished writing down everything, Laurel gave her staff a grateful smile. "Thanks for pitching in this way. I know Winnie is going to be very grateful."

BUSINESS WAS BRISK at the Cinnamon Stick from eleven until one-thirty. Then, just as they were experiencing their second lull of the day, an unexpected customer popped in. Jacqueline was dressed in jeans and a simple T-shirt, but even in such everyday wear she looked stunning.

Laurel gave her a closer look, searching for flaws. Unless it was possible to have teeth that were too white, she couldn't find any.

Then she scolded herself. Jealousy was a very unattractive emotion. *Be friendly. Smile.*

"Hi, Jacqueline."

"Hey, Laurel. Beautiful day, isn't it?"

Jacqueline slid up on a stool and Laurel marveled

anew at the length of her legs. When Laurel sat on those stools, her toes barely reached the ground. Jacqueline's boots—a serviceable tan color—were planted flat on the wood plank floor.

"I want to apologize about last night," Jacqueline announced.

"You do?"

"If I'd known Corb had a new girlfriend I would never have accepted Olive's invitation."

"Right. Well..." It was odd hearing herself described as Corb's girlfriend. But she was more than that now. She was his fiancée.

"I wasn't even expecting Corb to be there," Jacqueline continued. "Olive made it sound like it would be just the two of us and she seemed so sad and lonely, I couldn't say no."

Not only beautiful, but nice, too. Laurel could feel her smile tighten.

Then Jacqueline leaned in a little closer and lowered her voice. "Also, I wanted to reassure you that I haven't told anyone your news. Not about the baby or the engagement. Though I must admit both caught me by surprise."

Put Corb and herself in that camp, too.

"Thanks, Jacqueline. I appreciate your discretion. Let me get you a coffee and a cinnamon bun for the road."

"I won't say no."

While Laurel was pouring the coffee, Eugenia poked her head through the opening between the kitchen and the counter. She'd been in since eleven o'clock, first helping with the lunch hour, then making the soup for tomorrow's menu.

"Hello, stranger," she said cheerfully. "Haven't seen much of you lately."

"It's been a crazy summer." Jacqueline smiled ruefully. "Dad's leased a bunch more land and is working on expanding our herd. Not much time for making unnecessary trips to town."

"All work and no play…" Eugenia wagged a finger at her. It was clear that she liked Jacqueline and Laurel could understand why. Ten minutes later the other woman was on her way, having left Laurel lots to think about.

Why hadn't Corb wanted to marry her? She seemed perfect to Laurel. She was beautiful, not to mention kind and friendly. And she came from a ranching family so she would fit in at Coffee Creek Ranch perfectly.

No wonder Olive had invited her to dinner. If Laurel was Corb's mother, that's who she'd want her son to marry, too.

CORB CALLED LAUREL fifteen minutes after closing to see how she was doing. She'd just locked the door when her cell phone chimed.

"I'm fine," she assured him. It was true her stomach was queasy, but that was a feeling she was learning to live with.

Still, she was touched that he'd thought to call. As soon as she'd seen his name and number light up on the display, she'd felt her spirits lift. "Guess who dropped by to talk this afternoon?"

"Jacqueline?"

"Right on the first try," she said, a little surprised.

"She came by the ranch to see me, too."

Laurel's heart lurched a little to hear that. Jacqueline hadn't said anything to *her* about talking to Corb. "Oh, yeah? What time?"

"About an hour ago. I could smell cinnamon on her breath, so I figured she'd been to the café, first."

"You were close enough to smell her breath?"

He laughed. "Nah. I was kidding about that. She told me she'd spoken to you, apologizing for her awkward appearance at dinner last night. I told her it wasn't her fault—she had nothing to be sorry for. She was just trying to be kind to a grieving woman."

"Right." But Laurel wondered. Had the trip to the ranch really been necessary? Maybe Jacqueline's intentions weren't quite so admirable as she'd thought. After all, she'd dated Corb for five years, hoping the relationship would lead to marriage. It couldn't be easy for her to see him agreeing to marry someone else after such a short period of time.

"I imagine she told you that she's keeping our little secret?" Laurel asked.

"She did. Which is decent of her."

"Yes." She waited to see if he had anything more to say about Jacqueline. He was quiet for so long she wondered if their connection had been lost.

"Corb?"

"I'm still here."

"The line sounds funny."

"That's because I'm using my Bluetooth."

"So you're in your Jeep?"

"I am."

"Driving somewhere?"

"It's what I usually do in my Jeep."

Was she silly to hope? But she couldn't stop herself. She went to the window and parted the wooden slats for a view of the street, just in time to see his dusty Jeep slide into a parking space near the front door.

"Let me in?" he asked. And then the line went dead.

Laurel smiled and closed her phone, tucking it into the pocket of her jeans before unbolting the door and opening it wide.

Corb took one step, then gathered her in his arms and kissed her. Thoroughly. Not sweetly or tentatively, but as if he had only one thing on his mind and it didn't involve clothing.

He kicked the door shut with his booted foot, then kissed her again, somehow managing to release the clip holding up her hair at the same time.

"Wow, Corb…"

He smiled. "I was just thinking…. We did get the green light from the doctor…."

"That's true."

"Then how about we go upstairs?"

Her body was on fire. She needed no persuading. Taking his hand she led him up the staircase and into the upper apartment. She'd slept late that morning and hadn't bothered folding up the pullout coach. Or straightening the bedding.

"I'm sorry about the mess."

"What mess?" His eyes locked with hers, and then he kissed her again.

Chapter Nine

Corb hadn't driven to town planning to make love to Laurel. After Jacqueline's surprise visit to the ranch, his mother had cornered him for another little talk.

She'd helped him see that an elopement wasn't what the family needed right now. And his plan had been to open a discussion with Laurel about it.

But somehow, when she'd opened that door, kissing her had moved to the top of his agenda.

And he'd been blown away.

All fine and well to talk about getting married because it was "the right thing" to do.

But here was the baser truth. He wanted her.

He'd made a baby with this woman. Shouldn't he know what it felt like to make love to her?

And when she led him willingly upstairs, all rational thought left him. Maybe, in a corner of his mind, he hoped having sex with her would bring back memories of the night they'd conceived their baby.

It didn't happen, though.

He felt as if he was exploring the lush, magical wonders of her body for the very first time. Only at the end, when he was gazing into her flushed and smiling face, was there a whisper in the back of his head. *I've seen her like this before.*

He closed his eyes, waiting for more memories to come flooding in. When that didn't happen, he opened his eyes to find her watching him intently as if waiting for him to say something. But he stayed silent not wanting to admit that it hadn't worked. The past was still locked away in some isolated section of his brain.

When he gathered her into his arms to hold her close, he knew that he had done this the first time, as well. He felt her soft face pressed against his chest and he wondered what she was thinking.

And an odd question occurred to him.

How had he stacked up…compared to the first time?

"Corb?"

He hadn't had a headache all day. But suddenly he felt the familiar tension in his skull. He was happy holding her. Very happy. But he didn't want to talk. He didn't want to admit that even after making love to her, he still couldn't remember the time before.

He considered pretending he was asleep. But Laurel had already shifted up on her elbow and was looking at him. He studied her beautiful eyes, golden-brown and flecked with copper. His gaze shifted lower, to the freckles on her nose. Also copper. He kissed them.

"Are you okay?" he asked.

"Very okay. But I need to talk to you about something."

His gut tightened.

"I know you can't remember this—"

The tension in his head turned to a pulsing pain.

"—but that first week we spent together, you talked quite a bit about Jacqueline."

Jacqueline? Why the hell was she talking about Jacqueline?

"You sounded so done with her. So sure that you'd made the right decision not to marry her."

God help him, he had *no* idea where she was going with this. "It's true. Don't tell me you have a problem with that?"

"The only problem I have is believing you. I hadn't met her back then. Now that I have—well, Corb, frankly she's gorgeous. And nice and friendly. Plus she's a rancher, just like you. Wouldn't she fit in perfectly as your wife?"

He propped his head up and stared at her. "Did my mother somehow brainwash you into asking that?"

"Of course not."

"Are you trying to get out of our engagement? If so, just tell me. You don't have to try to rekindle my feelings for Jacqueline."

"No, no." She placed her hand against the side of his face. "I don't want out. I was afraid you felt trapped. Even before I met Jacqueline I was worried about that."

He took her hand from his face, and kissed it. "I imagine you feel trapped sometimes by the baby growing in your body."

The look she gave him was inscrutable. He wondered if she was thinking about her life back in New York City. He would never know exactly what she was giving up by staying in Montana and marrying him.

He wished he could have seen her there, even just once. To see how well she had fit in, how happy she'd been.

But maybe it was better this way. He could pretend that he was giving her everything she wanted, and not just selfishly taking over her life so he could be near their baby.

"So we're *both* trapped," she said. "Is that what you're saying?"

"I'm just being honest. You know we wouldn't be talking marriage if it wasn't for the baby. To say that we're trapped might be going too far. How does 'gently corralled' sound?"

AWFUL. IT SOUNDED just awful to Laurel. But she didn't say that. What was the point? Corb wasn't trying to hurt her. He was just being perfectly logical.

Which she hated.

She had wanted him to tell her he loved her. He'd been looking into her eyes as if he could see her very soul, and she'd longed to hear him say the words that were all but bursting to be free from her heart.

But he hadn't and so she'd held her words in, too. It hurt, though, knowing that she could well spend the rest of her life waiting for something that he might never tell her.

What would that be like? Living her life with a man who didn't really love her?

She already knew the answer to that.

"Laurel?" His voice was gentle. "Are you *sure* you're okay?"

She desperately wanted to say something funny, to ease the tension and take his focus off her. But for once her sense of humor let her down.

"I'm good, Corb. But hungry. We pregnant women

need to eat." At least she'd managed to lighten the mood a little. She could feel his muscles relax and see the relief in his eyes.

"Now that you mention food, my original plan was to take you out to dinner. I know a great place in Lewistown. Want to give it a try?"

"Gosh, I can't remember the last night I went out on the town. That sounds wonderful."

He got out of bed, giving her a nice view of his muscular cowboy body—still leaner than it had been two months ago. He hadn't put back all the weight he'd lost after the accident. She knew the story behind the scar on the left side of his abdomen. Also knew that when he turned around, his butt would be firm and round.

She'd tried to be subtle, but he noticed her checking him out. "What do you think?" He flexed his biceps. "Do I pass inspection?"

"Hmm." She tilted her head and put a finger to her lips. "Quite nice, but a little on the skinny side…"

He whooped, then tackled her, taking her right back onto the bed, where he leaned over her and kissed her firmly on the lips. "I may be scrawny, but I'm tough."

"Uncle," she conceded. When he'd released her she turned her back to him and slipped on her bra and top. She knew she had nice curves, but no one would ever call her skinny and she wasn't about to parade her body in front of him to invite his commentary.

But as she was zipping up her jeans, he came from behind her for a hug and planted a kiss on her neck. "You're a beautiful woman. And I feel like a very lucky man."

It wasn't *I love you*.

But it was very nice.

CORB TOOK HER to a restaurant that specialized in Montana beef and they both ordered a steak and salad. As they waited for their meals to arrive, Corb broached the subject of their wedding.

"What do you think about getting married right away?"

Laurel felt thrilled and panicked at the same time. "Really?"

"It's a good time for me right now. In another month I'll be so busy moving cattle I won't have time to think."

But was he taking enough time to think now? "We could wait until winter to get married. Would that be a better time?"

"I'm not a fan of waiting. Getting cold feet?"

"Not at all." Honestly? Yes. But she took comfort from the fact that Corb seemed so sure they were doing the right thing. "Want me to go online and look for flights to Vegas?"

He was quiet so long that she wondered if he'd heard her. But finally, he spoke. "About that. Are you dead set on eloping? Because I talked to my mother today. And she has other ideas."

"Oh, does she?"

He nodded, not seeming to sense the new tension in her voice. "Weddings are family matters. You don't mind if we let her have a little input?"

Yes, was her first, gut reaction. *I would mind.* But if she was hoping to have a decent relationship with her mother-in-law, it wouldn't be wise to antagonize her from the start.

"I suppose we could talk to Olive." What could it really hurt? With the recent death in the family, surely her mother-in-law would see that a quiet elopement was the best way to proceed.

AFTER THEY FINISHED dinner, Corb encouraged Laurel to order tea and dessert. She was surprised by this because he'd started checking his watch so often she'd assumed he was in a hurry to leave.

After the waiter headed for the kitchen with her request for peppermint tea and chocolate mousse, and Corb's coffee and brandy order, Laurel leaned across the table.

"Tell me more about what happens on a ranch during the fall season."

If she was going to be a rancher's wife then she had a lot to learn.

"Once we have the cattle in the pastures close to home, we have to sort and wean the cows and calves, doctor them up and get them preg tested."

She assumed he meant "pregnancy" tested. "Why do you do that?"

"To have an idea when the calves will be coming next spring—sometimes it's March, but it can be as late as April or May."

Her chores on the farm as a young girl had included feeding the chickens and collecting the eggs and that was pretty much it. Her father and his hired man had taken care of the fields and the cattle.

"Do you think you'd like to take an active role on the ranch? My mother always did."

"I'd need a lot of training, I guess."

He gave her a warm, approving smile. "I have a feeling you'll catch on quick."

Something beyond her field of vision seemed to catch his eye then. His intimate smile vanished, and he rose from his seat. Laurel noticed a woman at a nearby table glance at him, then look again.

Lick your lips, why don't you?

But Laurel didn't blame the woman for admiring the view. Corb was the finest-looking man in the room and any woman with a pulse would notice.

Laurel shifted to see who Corb was looking at. And wasn't it Olive, dressed in a tailored pantsuit and clutching a black patent bag. As she neared their table Corb commandeered a third chair.

"Hey, Mom, why don't you join us? We just ordered dessert."

Everything happened so fast that Laurel hardly knew what to think. Had the meeting been planned? She couldn't imagine why else Olive would have happened by their table at this moment.

But it turned out that Olive did have an explanation.

"I hope you don't mind if I interrupt, Laurel? I just finished a business dinner with an old friend of Bob's. He's interested in purchasing horses and he'd rather not wait for our fall auction."

"Not at all," Laurel said, while Corb signaled the waiter, who noticed the new addition to the table and quickly came to take Olive's order.

"Black coffee is fine for me." Olive gave her son a warm smile, then shifted her gaze to Laurel. "I understand congratulations are in order, dear."

Tacking on that "dear" at the end of her sentence was

a brilliant touch, Laurel thought. Corb noticed, too, and smiled. She could guess what he was thinking.

Good. Mom's warming up to her.

Laurel wished it could be true. But she had her doubts. She still felt a chill every time Corb's mother looked in her direction.

Never had a smile been so difficult to force. "Thank you."

Conversation paused as beverages and Laurel's chocolate mousse were delivered to the table. As soon as the waiter was gone, Olive said, "A baby. *And* a wedding. Quite a lot to celebrate. Too bad you can't drink or I'd order a bottle of champagne."

"It is exciting," Laurel agreed. "But also overwhelming—for me, and it must seem so to you, too."

"Well." Olive arched her finely drawn brows, which drew attention to her beautifully made-up gray-green eyes. "These things happen when we're not careful."

Laurel shot a glance at Corb, who stepped in quickly. "It's more my fault than Laurel's, Mom."

She was glad he'd defended her, but wished he'd simply declared the topic too private to discuss.

"Our baby may not have been planned, but he or she will be loved and wanted," Laurel said.

"But of course. By all of us. But first we must have the wedding."

What was that look passing between mother and son? Worried that she might be losing control of the conversation, Laurel stepped in quickly. "Given the unfortunate timing with your family's recent loss and everything, Corb and I thought a discreet elopement would be the best."

Olive couldn't argue with such a sensible plan, could she? And yet, she did.

"For sure, the timing could be better, but we're talking about the first wedding in our family. A big celebration is out of the question, but we simply must have a dinner for immediate family. Imagine how hurt Cassidy and B.J. would feel if they were excluded."

Laurel doubted that. Cassidy and B.J. had busy, happy lives of their own. And both of them liked to keep trips back to the family ranch down to the minimum. She hadn't known the family for long, but she had at least that much figured out.

No, this had to be about what Olive wanted.

And Corb?

She studied her cowboy's expression and wasn't mollified at his artless smile. He was pretending this had nothing to do with him. But she still couldn't help suspecting he had set her up.

"We could always have a party later, after the wedding." She wasn't giving up on the elopement plans without a fight. She and Corb *needed* that time, for just the two of them. Especially since he'd already explained there could be no honeymoon.

If they waited until later, after all the fall work was done, she'd be five months pregnant. And she wanted some time alone with him before that stage.

"It's *your* wedding," Olive said. "And you should certainly do whatever you prefer. I just thought that it would be nice for the family to have a happy reason to get together."

Olive lowered her eyes then, but not before Laurel had seen the sheen of unshed tears. Corb had noticed, too, because he reached across the table to cover his mother's hand with his.

"We aren't that set on our plans, are we?" His eyes were pleading with Laurel. *Look how upset my Mom is,* they seemed to say. *Won't you do this to make her happy?*

"Nothing is booked yet," she agreed, begrudging each word as she saw her lovely weekend with Corb dissolving into a gathering out at the ranch with his family.

"Well, then." Olive batted her tears away and produced a tentative smile. "That's fine then. You can get married at the ranch and save some money and we'll have a nice family get-together at the same time. How does that sound?"

Laurel shrugged and left the talking to Corb, who was quick to concur with his mother. Next thing she knew, Olive had removed her PDA from her purse and was looking at dates. "If you want to steer clear of the fall roundup, may I suggest Sunday of next week?"

"So soon?" Laurel voice squeaked, betraying her nervousness.

"Why not take the plunge and get it over with?" Corb countered.

Wow. How romantic. Really, Corb? Take the plunge and get it over with? "What about *two* weeks from next Sunday?" She didn't really care about the timing. She just wanted to feel like she had *some* input on the planning.

Olive considered the request, then nodded, as if it was her place to approve the date. "If it's a nice day, you can say your vows by the lake."

The fall colors would be at their peak by then. They'd have beautiful wedding pictures, at least. "Okay."

"And we can have lunch after, on the patio."

"I could ask Eugenia to cater," Laurel suggested.

"Whatever you want, dear." Olive's smile couldn't have been sweeter.

Laurel reached for her cup of lukewarm tea and downed half of it. Silently, she envied Corb the coffee and brandy that he'd ordered. If ever she could have used a drink, now was the time.

She'd just gone her second round with her mother-in-law-to-be. And come out the loser, again.

Chapter Ten

The next week passed in a whirl of planning and organizing. On Monday Corb and Laurel headed back to Lewistown to get their wedding license. They also purchased wedding rings—matching bands of eighteen-karat yellow gold.

On the drive back to Coffee Creek, Corb filled her in on how his calls to his siblings had gone.

Cassidy and B.J. hadn't been as surprised as Corb expected. He smiled at her ruefully. "I guess they remember all the stuff that I forget."

Laurel squeezed his hand, wanting him to think it didn't matter. She'd given up hoping, at this stage, that he'd ever remember anything of that special first week. And he must have done the same.

"Can they come?" she asked.

"Cassidy said she wouldn't miss it. B.J. was supposed to be heading out to a rodeo in Arizona, but he said he would withdraw his name."

Like Jackson, Corb's oldest brother, B.J., was a bit of an enigma to Laurel. Unlike Jackson, though, who tended to hang back at family gatherings, B.J. had a natural air of authority that she supposed came with being the firstborn. "How long has B.J. been on the rodeo circuit?"

"Since he was eighteen. Dad and Mom were both pretty choked up when he announced he was going on the road. He's made quite a name for himself, including several World Championships. But he hasn't had a fixed address for almost half his life now." Corb shook his head as if such a thing was unimaginable to him. "I keep thinking he's going to get tired and want to come home, but it hasn't happened yet."

"I bet your mother would be happy if it did."

"We all would. Especially with Brock gone."

"Do you think there's any chance your sister will come back to Coffee Creek when she finishes her degree?"

"She says no, but I have my doubts. You should see the way Cassidy is with animals. She has a special gift that'll be wasted if she decides to work at some accounting office all her life."

"Maybe she has a gift for accounting, too."

Corb gave her a look that told her what he thought about that idea. But maybe it wasn't her natural talents that were driving Cassidy from Coffee Creek. If Olive was *her* mother, Laurel figured she'd be looking to put at least a hundred miles between them, too.

But that wasn't kind. She had to stop thinking of Olive in such a negative way. The woman might have her flaws, but she was Corb's mother.

As they turned onto Coffee Creek's Main Street, Laurel asked if he had told Jackson about the wedding yet.

Corb's forehead creased with worry. "Been meaning

to. But it's like the guy is avoiding me. I am for sure going to track him down tomorrow morning."

He pulled up to the Cinnamon Stick, leaning over the gear shift to give her a kiss. "You haven't invited Winnie yet, have you?"

"I'm going to call her tonight," she promised, giving him one more smile before hurrying back to relieve the staff at the café.

Corb started to drive away, then paused and unrolled the passenger window. "Almost forgot to tell you. Mom says she set aside a dress for you at Sapphire Blue in Lewistown. Said to tell you that it would look great on you."

Really? Olive was selecting her wedding dress now?

Corb must have seen that she was annoyed. He gave her that *please be kind to my mother* look again. "Just try it on, sugar. Okay? You don't have to buy it if you don't like it."

WHEN LAUREL CALLED Winnie later that evening, she vented about the way Olive had taken over her wedding, right down to choosing her dress.

"You have to stand up to her. Or she'll walk over you for the rest of your life."

"I know. And believe me, I'd love to tell her where to shove her wedding plans. But then Corb gives me this look that I call his *please be nice to my mother look*. Honestly, Winnie, I can't resist him when he turns on his charm."

Winnie laughed. "Oh, you have it bad, girl. Real bad."

"I know. Just about the only thing that could make

this whole Coffee Creek Wedding thing tolerable for me, is if you could come. Do you think you can?"

"I'm so sorry, but no. I had another appointment today and the doctor was real stern. He said I could lose my baby if I wasn't careful."

Laurel told herself it was selfish to be disappointed. "You better listen to him."

"Believe me, I am. This baby…" Winnie's voice weakened, then grew stronger again. "At first I really resented being pregnant. But now I think I would have just dissolved with grief if it wasn't for Brock's baby. I'm going to love this child so much—" Her voice caught again. "I already do."

CORB COULD COOK when he had to. Besides eggs and bacon, he also made stew, in huge batches that he froze in plastic tubs on the top shelf of his freezer. He grabbed one of the tubs that evening when he finished work, transferred it to a roasting pan and stuck it in the oven to heat.

Then he went looking for Jackson. There were no lights on at his foster brother's place, so he figured Jackson must be at the office.

Corb made his way back to the home barn, pausing at the doorway to the office. Jackson was behind the desk, staring at the computer screen.

"Hey. Haven't you put in enough hours today? Come up to my place. I've got some stew in the oven and some cold ones in the fridge. I guarantee you one thing. You're not likely to get a better offer tonight."

He slipped into the upholstered chair across from Jackson's. "I have good news for a change."

"Yeah? I could use some."

"Laurel and I—we're getting married."

Jackson looked as stunned as if he'd pulled out a gun and threatened to shoot him. "Winnie's friend from New York? I thought you didn't remember her? That you'd forgotten pretty much everything that happened around the time of the accident."

"That's true, but let's keep that part between you and me, okay? The thing is—" He brushed his hands against his jeans. Telling B.J. and Cassidy his news over the phone had been a cinch compared to this. "The thing is, she's pregnant. It happened the night before—"

He stopped, not sure what to say. The night before the wedding that never happened? The night before the accident that took the life of his baby brother?

Jackson was staring at the ground. From the expression on his face, the same emotions were churning within him. But when he finally lifted his gaze, he had managed a small smile.

"You're right. That *is* good news. Congratulations, buddy."

As soon as she saw the exterior of the Blue Sapphire, Laurel could tell that the store catered to an older, wealthier clientele. The two-story, wooden Victorian had been painted a lovely, rich blue, with white trim. The display window had several smartly coordinated outfits with matching handbags and shoes.

More encouraging was a sign announcing a blowout sale with prices marked down from fifty to seventy-five percent.

If she had to buy a dress she didn't like, at least she'd be getting it at a good bargain.

Squaring her shoulders—all she'd promised was to try it on—she walked up the stairs and into the potpourri-scented shop.

Inside, three salesclerks were trying to keep up with the demands of about a half-dozen customers. "It's the first day of our sale," one of them explained to Laurel as she rushed by with her arms full of clothes, heading to the till to ring them up.

Laurel browsed through a rack of dresses as she waited to be helped. After only a few minutes, a woman in her fifties, stylishly dressed and very well-groomed, came up to her with a smile.

"Thanks for your patience. May I help you find something?"

"I'm getting married soon and my fiancé's mother spotted something here that she thought I would like."

"You must be talking about Olive Lambert."

When Laurel nodded, the older woman beamed.

"Olive is one of our best customers. I have the dress put away for you, dear." She put a hand on Laurel's back and led her to the curtained change rooms at the rear of the store. "My name is Lisa. You wait right here while I get the dress."

Less than a minute later she returned with a strapless sheath in an ivory silk with flattering ruching around the waist.

"This is our last one. I'll bet it's going to look fabulous on you. Olive has quite the eye."

Laurel examined the dress with begrudging admiration. It was actually quite nice.

Lisa hung the dress on the hook in the change room. "You call me if you need help with that zipper, okay?"

And then she was off, helping another customer.

Laurel pulled the curtain closed, then removed her T-shirt and jeans, taking off her bra, as well, so the straps wouldn't show. She had just put on the dress and was contorting her body in an effort to get the zipper all the way up, when she heard a familiar voice in the change room next to her's.

"Here, Mom, I found this for you to try on, too."

It was Jacqueline. Laurel was sure of it.

"Thanks, love," was the reply. "I sure hope one of these works. I hate shopping for dresses."

"Try this one first," suggested the woman who had helped Laurel earlier. Lisa. "Your daughter can sit here and wait, if she wants."

Laurel was about to step out to say hi to Jacqueline and to ask for help doing up the dress properly, when Jacqueline's mother said something intriguing.

"So are the rumors true? Help me with these buttons, love."

Amid rustling from the change room, Jacqueline said, "Which rumors?"

"Don't pretend you don't know what I'm talking about. Is Corb Lambert marrying that woman from New York City?"

Laurel sank into the chair, on top of her discarded clothing.

"Yeah. She was a lot smarter than me," Jacqueline replied. "She got pregnant."

Oh my God. Laurel stared at her reflection in the

mirror, horrified. And she'd thought Jacqueline was *nice*. Boy had she been fooled.

"You can't be serious. You wouldn't have—"

"No. Of course I would never have stooped that low. But the Lamberts, for all their unassuming ways, are one of the richest ranching families in Montana. So, I suppose it must have been tempting. For a certain type of woman."

Her mother tsk-tsked. Then there was the sound of curtain rings scraping against a metal rod. "Oh, that is totally awesome on you, Mom. You have to get that."

"I think I will. I'm not even trying on the others."

Thank God, Laurel thought. She needed them gone. And soon. Her phone beeped then, and she pulled it out of her purse to see a text message from Winnie.

Did you try on the dress? she'd asked. Is it awful?

Something was awful all right. But it wasn't the dress.

Laurel covered her face with her hands, and tried to compose herself. Even though she'd only met Jacqueline a few times, it still hurt to hear her pass on such malicious gossip. Probably what hurt the most, though, was the kernel of truth at the heart of it all. She, too, had felt as if she might be trapping Corb into this wedding.

But she'd given him the chance to back out, hadn't she?

And it wasn't as if this was any easier for *her*.

Laurel forced herself to take deep, slow breaths until she felt her heart rate level out to normal.

Then she pushed back the curtain.

Lisa was right there.

"Oh, my, look at that fit. It doesn't need a single alteration."

If she noticed the stunned expression on Laurel's face, maybe she put it down to shock at finding such a wonderful dress.

"Turn around, honey, and I'll get that zip...."

Obediently Laurel swiveled, and then felt the woman's warm fingers tug the zipper up the final inch.

"Lovely. Would you like a picture to show Olive?"

Laurel's phone had fallen to the floor at some point. Lisa picked it up and expertly snapped a couple of photos—obviously she was used to performing this service for her clients. Then she handed the phone back to Laurel.

"Olive will be so pleased. I've seen that dress on many women, but it's only been perfect on one of them—and that's you."

Obligingly Laurel texted the photo to Olive and Winnie. And she bought the dress. Olive replied right away. I was right! It's perfect. Laurel rolled her eyes, but she couldn't deny that it wasn't true.

She didn't hear back from Winnie until she'd returned home to the apartment over the Cinnamon Stick.

You look like a vision in that dress! read the text message. Did you buy it?

Laurel sat on the sofa, and punched in her reply. Yes. But I wish you'd been there. Oh, did she ever. She could just imagine her more assertive friend pushing back the curtains of that changing room and giving Jacqueline a good dressing-down. She might have done it herself if she hadn't been so shocked.

As if sensing Laurel's need to talk to her, Winnie didn't text a reply. She phoned instead.

"Are you okay?"

Laurel gushed out the story of what had happened at the dress shop.

"That bitch. I wish I had been there. I'd have torn a strip off her."

Laurel laughed, knowing this was no idle threat.

"She's just jealous, Laurel. Think about it. She dated Corb for *five years*. And you've known him for what— just three months?"

"Yeah, I know. But, she is right about one thing. Corb wouldn't be marrying me if I wasn't pregnant."

"Are you sure about that? This isn't the 1950s, Laurel. People don't *have* to get married anymore. There are all sorts of options. You and Corb are getting married because you're awesome together. So stop letting that woman get to you, okay?"

Laurel let the words sink in for a few seconds. "Winnie?"

"Yeah?"

"You're the best."

THURSDAY CORB WAS driving home from town with a case of beer, two bottles of champagne and a bottle of nonalcoholic wine for the wedding, when he noticed Maddie's old Ford puttering at half his speed on the road ahead of him.

He eased off the accelerator, not wanting to overtake her on the narrow country road. Going slower wasn't a bad idea anyway. He had a lot on his mind.

Like the wedding, which was a little over a week

away. He'd thought he would be nervous as the day grew closer. But he wasn't, and that confused him.

Also, he was thinking about Jacqueline. Laurel's questions the other night had stuck in his head and he found himself wondering why it was that just a few months ago the idea of getting married had seemed out of the question, whereas now, he was kind of excited about it.

Was it the baby? If Jacqueline had gotten pregnant, would he have felt okay about marrying her, too?

He didn't think so. But sorting out his true feelings for Laurel was difficult. He was too busy focusing on keeping her and the baby in Montana.

Brock was gone, but the Lambert family lived on, and so did Coffee Creek Ranch. His child was part of it—the family and the land were all part of a way of living that Corb treasured. Maybe one day his son or daughter would opt out the way Cassidy and B.J. had done.

But his child had to be given the choice.

Marrying Laurel was his chance to give their child that choice. And he didn't want to spend the rest of his life regretting that he hadn't taken action to make sure that happened.

Corb slowed as he approached the fork in the road. Ahead of him, Maddie turned on her indicator light and he watched as her taillights veered to the right. He took his foot off the accelerator and paused before splitting off in the opposite direction.

It struck him, suddenly, as strange that in all his life he'd never seen Silver Creek Ranch.

At the last moment he jerked his wheel to the right.

The approach to his mother's sister's place was not as well maintained as their road. His Jeep jostled over deep-set ruts, and he shook his head as he imagined what the road would be like when it rained. No wonder Maddie's truck was all beaten up.

He drove for six miles before he saw the homestead. A fieldstone house with a low roof, several barns and outbuildings, a series of corrals, all nestled into a clearing that overlooked a view of Square Butte, from a different angle than he was used to seeing it. The ranch was on a much smaller scale than the one where he'd grown up. But it was settled on a pretty piece of land, he conceded.

As he drove closer, he saw that the siding on the barns needed paint, some of the shingles on the roofs were lifting and the front windows of the house had been covered with aluminum foil.

Either Maddie was short on money or she was short on help. Either way, the place needed a little TLC.

Meanwhile, his unexpected appearance had been noted by the owner. Having parked her truck in front of the house, Maddie climbed out and took a stance with her legs planted firmly and her arms crossed. She was wearing work clothes, with a bandanna at her neck and a beat-up hat pushed back on her head. Clearly she was waiting to see what he wanted, why he had done this crazy thing and followed her home.

But he had no idea what his answer would be.

Maybe he should just pull a U-turn and head home like he should have done in the first place. Instead, he climbed out of the Jeep.

Two dogs came running, younger versions of Sky.

They'd spotted him, as well as their owner, and they looked at Maddie as if waiting for instructions. *Run him off the property? Or love him to bits?*

Maddie whistled, and they ran to her with impressive obedience. She put a hand on each of their heads. "Good girls," she said in a soft voice, never once taking her eyes off him.

He'd have to be the first to talk.

"Where'd you get those dogs? They look just like our dog, Sky."

"That's because they have the same lineage. Trixie and Honey are quite a bit younger than Sky, though."

Again, he was taken aback by her voice, which didn't match her rough-and-tumble appearance. And then he realized something else, too. Her voice was a lot like his mother's.

"So, you and Dad got your dogs from the same breeder?"

"I suppose you could say that."

He narrowed his eyes, trying to figure out what she was saying, or, more accurately, *not* saying. And then the lightbulb went on. "Sky was born here, on Silver Creek Ranch."

She didn't answer but Corb knew he was right.

"Did Dad buy her from you?" He'd seen his father walk right by Maddie Turner in town, not acknowledging her existence by as much as a glance in her direction.

"Corbett, you have a lot of questions all of a sudden. Why don't you leave things be? After all these years, the answers don't matter anymore."

"Just tell me one thing then. Why do you keep leaving fresh flowers on Brock's marker?"

She pressed her fingers to her right temple, as if trying to stop a secret throbbing. "Your brother wasn't as obedient as the rest of you kids. I'm sure he knew he wasn't supposed to talk to me. But he did anyway."

This rang true for Corb. Of all of them, Brock would be the one most likely to disobey the unwritten family rule. "When you ran into one another in town, you mean?"

"It started that way. But when he got older, he started dropping by the ranch every now and then." She nodded toward a stack of new shingles. "He was planning to fix my roof for me after the wedding."

Corb was speechless. All he could think of was his mother and how crushed she would be if she knew this. He already felt guilty just for driving here and talking to Maddie. But another part of him felt badly for Maddie, too.

"You're wondering if you should help me with the roof now that Brock's gone," Maddie said. "I can see it in your face. You don't hide your emotions very well. You're like your father that way."

Again the woman shocked him. This time by how well she seemed to know his father. Corb realized there was a lot of family history that he had no clue about.

"Did you know my dad well?"

She smiled sadly at that, then waved him off. "Go home, Corb. I've got hands to help me with this roof. And your loyalty belongs with your mother."

Chapter Eleven

Corb wanted to hole up in his cabin for the rest of the evening. Fry up some eggs and bacon, relax and watch the sunset. Maybe later, when it got dark, he'd call Laurel to talk over the day's events.

But his sense of responsibility wouldn't let him. So when he got back to the ranch, he headed for the office in the barn to work on the schedule for the next four weeks. It was a job he should have tackled a few days ago and he knew he wouldn't sleep well until it was done.

He was updating the spreadsheet on the computer when his mother appeared carrying a tray with dinner.

"I saw the light on," she said. "It's late, Corb—have you eaten?"

"No, but that sure smells great."

"Bonny made her enchilada casserole. Enough for at least a dozen people. She hasn't adjusted her recipes even though she's only cooking for one, now."

The plate, piled high with layers of spicy chicken, corn tortillas, salsa and cheese, was calling out to him. But his mother's words broke his heart and dulled his appetite.

He knew there was no sense reminding her that even when Brock was alive, they'd mostly eaten their evening meals at their own cabins. She was probably thinking back to the old days, when his dad was still alive and there were four kids—five when you included Jackson—around the table with her.

She'd gone through a lot of adjustments over the years. One by one, everyone had left her. That must be how she felt, anyway.

"How are you holding up, Mom?"

She managed a smile. "You've been so patient with me, son. But I am feeling stronger. Maybe planning this wedding of yours was just what I needed. It hasn't been overwhelming, since the affair is so small, but it's given me something to look forward to. Including having Cassidy and B.J. back home for a while."

Hoping he wasn't pushing his luck, but knowing that these warm moments between him and his mother didn't come along all that often, he decided to ask some questions.

"Mom, what's the deal between you and Maddie Turner? What happened to cause the rift between you two?"

In a flash it was as if his mother had become a different person. Her smile vanished and her face looked haggard and pained in the shadows cast from the overhead lighting.

"Why are you bringing that up?"

"I've—" He sensed it wouldn't be wise to mention anything about the wreath, or the border collies who were related to Sky, or the stack of shingles Brock had been meaning to replace. "I've run into Maddie a few times in town lately. It just seems strange the way we both act as if we don't even know the other one exists."

"Oh, Corb." His mother sighed, then sank into the upholstered chair. "I don't like to speak of it. I thought your father told all you kids this years ago."

He hadn't. He'd never said a word to explain the weird family divide. But again, Corb judged it was best to keep quiet and let his mother speak.

"I loved my father very much. He was a wonderful man, your grandpa Turner. But unfortunately Maddie was always jealous of me—I don't want to sound vain, but I was widely considered the pretty one, and it may be that my father favored me because I took after my mother. She died in childbirth, as you know."

"Yes." That much of the family history, he had been told.

"Maddie's jealousy got worse after I was married. She did her best to come between Father and me. So much so that she didn't even tell me when he had his stroke."

"Why would she do that?" Maddie had looked sad and lonely, but she hadn't struck him as mean. And what his mother described was more than mean. It was almost vicious.

"Who knows? Maybe she was worried I would talk him into changing his will. He left her the best and biggest share of the ranch, you know. Or maybe it was just jealousy, pure and simple. She'd always wanted all of Daddy's attention…."

There were tears in his mother's eyes, and Corb was sorry he'd raised the subject. He went to give her a hug and asked if he could walk her back to the house.

"No, I'm fine, dear. Stay here and eat your dinner then go home and get some rest." She placed a hand on his cheek.

"Thanks, Mom."

She paused on her way out the door. "Just please don't mention that woman to me ever again. Because of her, I never had a chance to say goodbye to my father or tell him one last time how much I loved him. And I will never forgive her for that."

An hour later, Corb finished with the schedule and closed up the office for the night. Outside the night air was cool and refreshing. He decided to leave the Jeep and walk the half mile to his cabin. He needed to clear his head and a sky dazzling with stars and a quarter moon was offering enough light for him to watch his footing.

Ten minutes later, he was almost at the first cabin when he heard a vehicle approaching from his rear. He moved to the side of the road and watched as Jackson slowly drove by, giving him a slight wave before turning into the driveway.

In the days prior to the accident, he'd run into Jackson several times during the day. Besides having breakfast together at the main house, they'd cross paths as they worked in the barns or out in the field with the cattle.

But since Corb had been released from the hospital, seeing Jackson was about as rare as a sighting of the shy northern bluebird.

Corb followed the truck, catching up to Jackson just before he went in the door to his cabin.

"Hey there."

Jackson turned. He looked weary, from the set of his shoulders, to the lines bracketing his mouth and weighing down his forehead.

"Hey, Corb. Out for a walk? Nice evening."

"Haven't seen you around the last few days."

"Been busy."

Corb waited, expecting to be invited in for a beer. When he wasn't, he headed for one of the willow chairs on the porch. "Mind if we sit for a while?"

Jackson didn't look pleased, but he took the other chair. He removed his hat and started tracing the rim with the pad of one thumb.

"What's been keeping you so busy lately?"

"Getting the horses ready to move the cattle. Have you worked up the schedule yet?"

"Just did that tonight. I've been wanting to talk to you about something else, though. I was wondering if you would be willing to take over the entire quarter horse breeding end of the operation. We could hire an accountant to handle some of the office work. And maybe an extra hand to look after the working horses."

"That would suit me fine," Jackson admitted. "But it doesn't feel right to take over Brock's job."

"Don't think of it that way."

"How the hell should I think of it?" Jackson's words came out in a rush of anger. "Lately I've been considering my options. It might be healthier for everyone concerned if I found a job somewhere else."

Corb stared at him, feeling as if he'd been sucker punched. "Have you been talking to other ranchers in the area about this?"

Jackson wouldn't look at him, just kept working at his hat. "I've had a few conversations."

That was the last straw. "Damn it, Jackson. I can't believe this. I've lost one brother and now you want to make it two?"

"Don't think of it that way." Jackson was mocking him, throwing back his own words.

Corb sprang out of the chair and went to lean on the railing. "Dad always treated you like one of the family. You've been with us for almost fifteen years now. But you're going to pack your bags as if we were just another job. Is that it?"

"No. Damn it, no. You must understand why I have to go."

Suddenly Corb's anger vanished. Jackson was acting out of guilt and there was no uglier feeling. "No, I do not. Running away won't change anything. And it'll sure make things worse for me. Besides being my best friend, I need you here. You're a talented horseman and I'd be hard-pressed to replace you with two men, let alone one."

Jackson joined him by the railing and offered him his hand. "I'm sorry. I should never have said all that. I owe you and this place my loyalty."

"If that's all it is, just loyalty, then maybe you *should* leave."

"No. I feel the same way about you, like you're my brother. And I felt the same about Brock. That's what makes it so hard."

"It is hard," Corb agreed. "But it's going to get better. And life goes on. You'll see."

"Speaking of life going on…" Jackson swallowed,

like he was nervous or something. "You heard from Winnie Hayes lately? Is she planning to come to the wedding?"

"Laurel invited her, of course. But apparently she's not well enough to travel."

Jackson looked sick when he heard this. "Do you know what's wrong?"

"I asked Laurel, and she said it was up to Winnie to fill us in on her health. She was real mysterious about it all."

"I hope it's not serious."

"Laurel didn't give me that impression. I told Mom she should call the Hayes family and check in with Winnie, but as far as I know, she hasn't done that yet." He paused then added, "Maybe you want to give her a call?"

"I doubt she wants to hear from me."

Corb didn't argue the point. For all he knew, Jackson was right.

THE IRONIC THING about planning a wedding, Laurel soon discovered, was that you had no time to spend alone with the man you were intending to marry. That weekend Olive wanted to go over the menu with the caterer, so Laurel agreed they would meet at the ranch at two o'clock on Saturday afternoon.

"Why don't you come, too?" she asked—well, more like pleaded with—Corb on the phone.

"I promised Jackson I'd help him shoe some horses today, or I would. Nothing I'd like better than to talk recipes with you and my mom."

Laurel laughed. "You liar."

She called Eugenia next, letting her know the time of the meeting and also suggesting that she come prepared with some choices for a casual outdoor barbecue.

Southwestern cuisine would be perfect for their low-key, family wedding, Laurel thought. But that was before Olive had her say.

Olive greeted them both at the door, then led them to the dining room table. Once they were seated, Eugenia handed out the menus she had printed off for the meeting. Corb's mom took one glance at the menu of ribs, baked beans, salads and corn bread, then set it aside and opened a red leather-covered notebook of her own. Slender gold pen in hand, she flipped through the pages until she found what she wanted.

"What about a shrimp salad to start?"

From her end of the table, Eugenia cast a worried look at Laurel, then focused again on Olive. "I can make a shrimp salad. That's no problem. But I thought we were going for a casual afternoon barbecue?"

"Really?" Olive already had perfect posture, but she managed to pull an extra inch out of her spine as she turned to look at Laurel. "Is that what you want, dear?"

"Everyone loves a good barbecue, don't they?"

"But this is an *occasion,* dear. Don't you want something special?"

She really didn't. But half an hour later Laurel had agreed with every one of Olive's menu suggestions, and the result was a French-inspired four-course meal.

"Are you sure you know how to cook all that stuff?" Laurel asked Eugenia as she walked her out to her car, leaving Olive in the dining room savoring her victory. "I sure couldn't."

"I can make anything—if I have the recipe. And they have plenty of those on the internet." Eugenia patted her hand. "Don't you worry—everything will be delicious."

On Sunday Olive insisted on having Laurel to dinner so they could discuss more wedding details. This time Corb was present, and Laurel noticed he was wearing his lucky shirt.

"This should be fun, huh?" she whispered in his ear as he bent to kiss her hello.

"Oh, yeah…" he said in a voice that denied the truth of the words. "More fun than deworming hogs in the springtime."

"Have you ever done that?"

"Nope. But I'd be willing to give it a try if I could get out of this."

Since Bonny didn't work on the weekend, Olive served reheated frozen pizza on china plates, with a salad starter—the kind that came in a package at the grocery store. Laurel picked up her silver fork and had to credit Corb's mother. She knew how to make fast food look good.

They'd barely finished eating when Olive pulled out the red leather notebook. First she went over color scheme suggestions for the flowers and the table linens. As soon as she said the words "table linens" she lost Corb. Laurel could see him craning his neck for a look at the baseball game playing silently in the family room.

Laurel was a fan of green, but Olive cringed when she mentioned this, suggesting instead a palette of white and silver.

"Okay," Laurel conceded. "We'll go with a white-and-silver color scheme. And for the flowers, I've always loved carnations. I know they're simple, but that's what I like about them."

"Oh, but freesia and white roses would be so much more elegant."

Seriously? Could she not get her way on something as simple as a carnation? She gave Corb's leg a surreptitious nudge.

He winced, then sat up straight, and reengaged with the discussion. "What's that?"

"Flowers, Corb," his mom said patiently. "Don't you think white roses and freesia would be nice?"

"Yes, but white carnations are elegant, too. And much cheaper," Laurel pointed out.

Corb looked from his mom to Laurel, then back to his mother. "Can't we have all of them? The roses, that free stuff and the carnations, too?"

Olive gave him a condescending smile. "But the carnations would just detract." She shifted her gaze to Laurel. "You see that, don't you, dear?"

Laurel sighed. Did she really care about the flowers that much? No, she did not. "Whatever, Olive. Let's just leave it in your hands. That is, if Corb agrees?"

"Uh-huh," he said, eyes back on the TV.

Olive looked pleased, then moved on to the next item on her list. "We'll need to have a few speeches during dinner. I know you kids want to keep things simple, so we won't go overboard. Just a toast to the bride— perhaps you'd like to do that, Corb? After which I'd like to say a few words."

Of course she would. Laurel couldn't imagine a situation where Corb's mother *wouldn't* like to say a few words.

"*I* have to make a speech?" Corb looked like he'd rather face down a rattler. Or maybe a rabid dog.

"I can get you a book on toasts for weddings from the library," Laurel suggested. "To give you some ideas."

"A book? They must have an app for that."

"Probably." But she'd been looking for an excuse to check out the local library and this seemed like a good one.

After coffee and a slice of the bumbleberry pie Laurel had brought from the café, Olive finally closed the notebook.

"That was a very productive evening, don't you think?"

"I do," Laurel agreed, not sure if she should laugh or cry. Basically Olive had just overridden her on every single decision to do with the wedding, while Corb obliviously watched it happen.

Was this what the rest of her life was going to be like?

Or would Corb *ever* pick her side over his mother's?

Later, as Corb walked her out to her car, she shook her head. "That was interesting. Any chance you might change your mind about eloping?"

Corb looked worried. "But planning our wedding has really been good for her. She actually seemed like her old self tonight. And this afternoon she took the new palomino out for a ride. It's the first time she's been on a horse since the accident."

"That's good," Laurel had to admit.

They'd reached her car. But instead of opening the door, Corb backed her right up against it and planted his arms on either side of her. Then he leaned in for a nice, thorough kiss. "Can I talk you into staying? A sleepover would be nice...."

She was tempted. A night in Corb's arms might help all of this make sense again. Lately she'd felt as if she was on a treadmill and couldn't find the pause button.

Much as she'd tried to shake the conversation she'd overheard between Jacqueline and her mother, certain phrases still haunted her.

She got pregnant.... I would never have stooped that low.

She knew Winnie was right, that Jacqueline was speaking out of envy. But for some reason those words still stung. And she couldn't keep asking Corb if he was sure about marrying her. He'd start to think that it was *her* who wasn't sure, and that was the one thing she did know for certain.

She loved Corb.

She loved him like crazy.

Placing her mouth close to his ear, she whispered in her sexiest kitten voice, "What will your mother think?"

Corb laughed. "I admit there are times when I humor my mother—but our sex life will never be one of them. Besides—" he pulled her in nice and close so she could feel the hard refuge of his chest, the solid beating of his heart "—why do you think I wore my lucky shirt?"

Chapter Twelve

As soon as they were alone in Corb's cabin, there was no bothering with the niceties. Corb shut the door, pressed Laurel's back to the solid oak and unleashed his passion with the hottest kisses she'd ever experienced.

She loved his strength; she loved his ardor. And she absolutely adored the way he scooped her into his arms and carried her up the stairs to the loft as if she were a delicate damsel in distress.

He truly was the sexiest man she had ever known, and he was all hers. She could see it in his eyes, the way they burned for her, just as she was burning for him.

They kissed again, only this time they also tugged at each other's clothes, peeling back the layers, until they were skin to skin.

They made love in a tangle of desperate need, without the tentativeness of the other two times. She knew his sweet spots, and, oh my, he knew hers.

Later, he pulled her in close and traced lazy patterns with his fingers on her tummy.

"There's a baby in here. Hard to believe, huh?"

Her heart swelled at the awe in his voice. "Our own little tadpole."

"I'm so excited, Laurel. I mean it. I want to do all the things with our child that my dad did with me."

"Such as…?"

"Go fishing. Teach him to ride. Give him his first horse."

"And if he's a she?"

"The list won't change. Dad did all those things with Cassidy, too. But he did spoil her some, as well. She was the only one of the kids who got a dog for her birthday."

"I expect you'd spoil a daughter, too."

"No doubt I would." He kissed her tummy, then kissed her lips. "Thank you for agreeing to marry this Montana cowboy when you probably had your sights set on a sophisticated New Yorker."

"I never thought about it that way. I guess I just hoped I would find someone I could share my life with, someone to love and to raise a family with."

"Well, you found him." He kissed her again. "I won't be one of those hands-off kinds of fathers, either. Diapers, 2:00 a.m. feedings, marathon rocking sessions— you can count me in on all of that."

Laurel sighed, and cuddled in closer to his solid warmth.

This was such a perfect moment. Of course, the icing on the cake would have been if he'd mentioned how much he loved *her*. Or some of the things he wanted to do together, as a couple.

But a lot of cakes tasted just fine without icing.

IF LAUREL THOUGHT the wedding plans had been squared away that weekend, she was wrong. On Tuesday Eugenia insisted on going over the recipes she'd found on the internet. Then on Thursday Olive phoned her in a panic about the wedding cake. She'd forgotten all about it. Had Laurel ordered one?

She hadn't.

In stepped Vince Butterfield, who must have overheard her talking on the phone to Olive, then later ranting to Dawn.

"Where am I going to get a wedding cake on such short notice?"

"I really don't know." Poor Dawn seemed as distressed as if it were her own wedding. "Maybe you could make one yourself?"

"I'll do it," said a masculine voice from the back room.

At first Laurel wasn't sure she'd heard Vince correctly. She pushed through the door to the kitchen, where she found him pulling the last batch of cinnamon buns out of the oven. How a man in cowboy boots, jeans and a big white apron managed to avoid looking silly, she didn't know. But Vince pulled off the look, looking both competent and hygienic, and completely masculine all at the same time.

"Did I hear that right? Vince, did you offer to bake a wedding cake for Corb and me?"

He nodded, setting down the pan on a hot pad, then shutting the oven door with the tip of his boot.

"Have you made a wedding cake before?"

"Nope."

She stood in the kitchen, not sure what to ask next, or if she should maybe make some suggestions, like no fruitcake please, or go easy on the rosettes and the thick white icing. Vince didn't seem to be awaiting any instructions, however.

"Leave it to me. You and Corb, you've got enough on your hands."

What did he mean by that? she wondered. But Vince had already said a lot of words for one morning. As he turned back to his baking, she knew better than to try and get anything more out of him.

IT WAS FRIDAY by the time Laurel made it to the library. She hadn't seen Corb since the night they'd spent together the previous Sunday. The wonderful chemistry of their lovemaking, and the tender hour Corb had spent holding her and talking afterward, had reassured her at the time that they were doing the right thing.

But after five days with no contact—other than texting and the occasional phone conversation—she was getting nervous again. She wanted to blame Jacqueline, but she suspected that she would be feeling the same way even if she hadn't overheard that conversation.

While their night together had been wonderful, he still hadn't told her he loved her. At the time, she'd felt it didn't matter. He was *showing* her how he felt. And cowboys weren't exactly famous for sharing their feelings.

Vince was a prime example of that.

But she wasn't marrying Vince, and she couldn't help needing more reassurance than Corb seemed prepared to give her. As the days to the wedding ticked by, and Sunday loomed closer, it seemed to her that he might have said the words *at least once*. If he felt them.

She pulled open the door to the library, which was

situated in a white clapboard building that had once been the town schoolhouse. Back in the forties and fifties, all the children in the area had been schooled together in this place. Framed black-and-white pictures on the wall in what had once been the cloakroom showed neat rows of wooden desks, with the smallest desks lined up to the teacher's left and the larger ones on the right. She couldn't imagine what it must have been like for one teacher to juggle all the grades in one room, but clearly that was how it had been done.

"Hello! Welcome!"

She followed Tabitha's voice into the main room. Here all the desks had been replaced with bookshelves. A metal desk sat in one corner, next to a computer and some filing cabinets. Across the room were a couple of wooden tables, with two more computers for the public to use. Presently both were vacant. It seemed she was the only patron in the library.

"For a change, I get to be the one to serve you," Tabitha said with a smile.

"Yes. I'm embarrassed that I've been in town for this long without visiting the library before now. I'm certainly not the regular customer that you are at the Cinnamon Stick."

Tabitha laughed. "Well, I am addicted to Vince's blueberry muffins. And the coffee is good, too."

"I'm glad—but why do you only visit us in the mornings? I've never seen you come in for lunch."

"Hasn't anyone told you? It was part of my divorce settlement."

"Pardon?"

"You know Burt and I used to be married?"

"I do."

"We used to go to the café together. Sometimes for breakfast and sometimes for lunch. When we separated, I got breakfast and he got lunch. Does it make sense now?"

"Yes. It makes perfect sense." It was lovely and heartbreaking all at the same time. But what had gone wrong between these two gentle souls? "You'll probably find this funny, but a few times I've thought to myself that the two of you would make a good couple."

"Well, it was true for a while. But it's never a good thing for a marriage when one partner does all the loving."

"Oh. I guess not." Laurel waited, wondering which had loved more and which had loved less. But Tabitha was finished confiding for the day.

"So," she prompted. "May I help you find something or are you just here to browse?"

"I'd love some help. I'm looking for a book with examples of wedding toasts."

"Ah!" Tabitha beamed. "That's right. Tomorrow is the big day, isn't it?"

And then, so subtly Laurel wasn't sure if she was imagining it, Tabitha checked out Laurel's waistline.

She knows I'm pregnant?

How was that possible? She hadn't even told Vince or Dawn, and she was pretty sure Eugenia had kept the news quiet.

Which left Jacqueline. Despite her promise to keep their news to herself, she must have talked. Silly her to be surprised.

If Jacqueline was blabbing about her in a dress shop

in Lewistown, she wouldn't have drawn the line about spreading the word here in Coffee Creek.

Not that it really mattered what people knew. In a few months she wouldn't be able to keep her secret anymore. But she sure hoped the whole town didn't see the affair the same way that Jacqueline did—as some sort of ruse to get Corb to marry her.

Laurel left the library with the book of wedding toasts under her arm, no longer certain that Corb was going to need it.

"WINNIE, WERE YOU nervous the night before your wedding?" Laurel was sitting on the floor in the apartment, sipping ginger ale and wishing, badly, that she could add something a lot stronger to the glass.

It was seven o'clock on Saturday evening. She'd received a text from Corb a few hours earlier telling her that Cassidy and B.J. had both arrived at the ranch. They were going to have a big welcome-home dinner, and did she want to join them?

She'd begged off, claiming there was too much for her to do to get ready for tomorrow.

And there *had* been a lot to do, but she'd done none of it. She hadn't filed her nails or painted her toenails. She'd also planned to have a bath and give herself a mini facial. Also not done. She hadn't even taken her dress out of the garment bag she'd brought home from the shop.

She was freaking out.

She wished Winnie was here, in person. But Winnie was at home with her feet up, doing her best to keep the baby that she and Brock had made together.

"I was more excited than nervous," Winnie said now, which did not make Laurel feel better *at all*.

"Oh."

"Are you okay, Laurel?"

"Yes. No. Oh, Winnie, what if I'm making a terrible mistake?"

"I don't know what to say to that. Other than to follow your heart. Do you love him, Laurel?"

"Yes."

"Well then? Seems pretty simple to me. Look, sweetie, I'm sorry but I've got to go. I haven't had the best day, myself."

Laurel felt like the most insensitive person possible. All her talk about the wedding must be bringing back so many painful memories for Winnie.

"I'm sorry. I've been so busy thinking of myself. I haven't been a very good friend to you, lately, have I?"

"Don't say that. You're a terrific friend. I just have bad days, when I can't help—" The rest of her sentence was lost as she choked over a soft sob.

"Go ahead and cry, Winnie. I'm sure a few tears won't hurt your baby."

And Winnie did cry. But only for a minute. Then she spoke again, her voice fortified with determination. "I'm going to rest now, Laurel, and I want you to go to sleep, too. Things will look brighter in the morning. I know your wedding is going to be beautiful. Try not to worry and just enjoy it."

Don't hang up, Laurel wanted to plead. But she knew it wasn't fair to keep Winnie from her rest when there wasn't anything her friend could say to help her, anyway. This was Laurel's life and her decision to make.

"Thanks, Winnie. We'll talk soon."

Laurel put away her phone, then eyed the pullout couch, which was all made up and ready for her to crawl into. But she knew she would never sleep. Instead she went to the suitcase she'd packed almost three months ago, when she'd thought she was coming to Coffee Creek for just a week.

No matter where she went in life, even if it was just a weekend away in the country, Laurel always took a velvet-covered box with her. It was about as big as a legal-sized envelope and two inches deep. Inside she kept her family—or what was left of them.

A picture of her and her mom taken when Laurel was two years old. She was sitting on her mother's lap and her mother was looking at her with such tenderness that it always brought a tear to Laurel's eye. She did remember her mother, but looking at this picture helped keep those memories strong.

Also in the box were her parents' wedding bands— one of which, the larger one, had about ten years more wear and tear than the other. She held them in her hands and wondered about her parents' wedding day. She knew they'd loved one another deeply. But had her mother felt any nerves the night before?

If only she could ask her.

The final item in the box was a letter. She didn't often read it. It made her too sad. But on this momentous night, she felt she needed to see those words again.

The letter was from her father—written in his familiar scrawling style. It had been left with his lawyer, along with his will, to be given to her in the event of his death.

The single page was wrinkled from repeated readings—and more than a few tears that had spilled from her eyes.

She took a deep breath. Then plunged on.

Dear Laurel, If anything should happen to me, I want you to let Mr. Wilson sell the farm on your behalf. He'll take care of everything and you'll be left with enough money to put you through college and maybe buy yourself a house later, or help you through any rough patches you encounter later in life.

I'm sorry I wasn't a better father. I did try to do my best, and you made it easy on me. You were a good kid and I thank you for that. Remember your mother, always. She loved you so much.
Dad

No matter how many times Laurel read the letter, it always wounded. Not that she hadn't known, growing up, that her father didn't love her. He was a kind man and he always made an effort, but there was always a faraway look in his eyes when she spoke to him that made him seem as if he wasn't really present.

She'd tried so hard to make him happy. She'd earned good grades at school. Learned how to cook and do laundry and help keep their home neat. She'd never indulged in "moods" and tried to say funny things to make him smile at the end of a long day spent in the fields or handling the cattle.

And what had been her reward?

You made it easy for me...thanks for that.

She'd wanted love. Not gratitude.

And her father had only wanted…release. He'd waited until she was eighteen. He'd waited until she'd graduated from high school, and then he'd died in an automobile crash.

Later, the police told her that they couldn't determine the reason he went off the road that day. He must have fallen asleep at the wheel.

But she'd known the truth. His promise to her mother fulfilled, her father had wanted to die that day.

It had been duty, not love, that bound her father to her. *Just like Corb.*

Laurel's heart started pounding too fast, her breathing was off. Putting a hand to her chest, she wondered why she hadn't seen the parallel earlier, between that early parental relationship and this new one with Corb.

If he was marrying her out of duty and not love, then one day she might have to expect a letter like this one from him.

Thanks for being cheerful and funny and making our years together easy. But I think it's time we went our separate ways….

What was it Tabitha had said? It wasn't a good thing for a marriage if one partner did all the loving. Had she shared that bit of wisdom with her because she suspected that Laurel and Corb were about to make the same mistake that she and Burt had made years ago?

She'd asked Winnie if she was making the right decision, but all she'd had to do was open her eyes. The signs were everywhere that she hadn't. Even in the way that Corb always put Olive's wishes ahead of hers.

She'd kept telling herself that it didn't really matter.

Only, one day, there would come a disagreement that was important to her, and when she needed her husband to have her back. But by then, the precedent would already be set. Olive's wishes came first. Hers second.

She'd spent the first eighteen years of her life trying to earn the love of a man and failing. Did she really want to repeat that mistake with Corb?

Laurel sat at the kitchen for a long while, trying to work out what she had to do. End it now?

Her heart shrieked *No.*

Maybe she should give Corb one more chance to prove that he really did care. Before she could change her mind, she dialed his cell phone. Even before he spoke, she could hear the sounds of conversation and laughter in the background.

"Laurel? Did you change your mind? Are you coming over?"

"No. Actually, I was hoping you could come here. I really need to talk to you right now."

"Tonight?" There was a pause for a second. In her mind she could picture the torn expression that would be on his face. "But Mom made this big meal. And with Cassidy and B.J. home, it doesn't feel right to run out on everyone."

"I see."

"Please change your mind and come over. We can grab some time for ourselves later on, once everyone's had dessert and coffee."

Maybe a reasonable person would have said yes. But

Laurel didn't have it in her to be reasonable tonight. This, on top of everything else, just seemed like too much.

"I don't think so, Corb. It's just too late."

"It's only eight," he said.

But she wasn't talking about the time.

Chapter Thirteen

Corb had made certain that Sky was at the main ranch house when Cassidy arrived home for the weekend. His sister had given their mother a kiss, then dropped to her knees and thrown her arms around the dog.

"Oh, you good girl. You haven't forgotten me, have you?"

The adoration in Sky's dark eyes was her answer and they'd been inseparable ever since. Corb guessed that Cassidy had even let Sky sleep on her bed—a definite no-no in this house when they'd been growing up.

They'd all gone to bed late last night. And now, a few hours before the wedding, Corb checked in at the house thinking lunch would be a good idea, since he hadn't had any breakfast. He found Cassidy curled up on the sofa eating a sandwich, Sky at her feet, accepting the odd discreetly offered piece of chicken or cheese.

His sister looked good, he thought. She'd always been cute. A long-legged blonde with the kind of skin that tanned easily every summer, and the greenest eyes of all of them, she'd never gone through an awkward adolescent stage that he could recall.

But now, in the final semester of her MBA, his sister was starting to look like a woman. The transition was kind of scary and he wondered how his mom felt about it.

Corb took his plate loaded with chicken sandwiches and carrot sticks and sank on the sofa next to her.

"So? Any men in your life these days, sis?"

"When I get engaged, I'll let you know." Having grown up with only brothers, Cassidy knew better than to give him a straight answer.

"That's a lot of sandwiches on your plate," B.J. commented, entering the room after his own foray into the luncheon buffet set out on the dining room table.

Cassidy and Jackson had done the work of making sandwiches, chopping veggies and piling Bonny's homemade cookies onto a plate. Their mother was still in her room, claiming to need the rest to prepare for the busy day to come.

"I'm surprised you have an appetite, considering that in less than two hours you're going to be signing your life away." B.J. settled into the big leather armchair that had once been their father's, and that everyone but him still did their best to avoid.

"If you knew Laurel, you'd understand why I'm not nervous," Corb retorted. Lobbing insults and challenging statements to his big brother was habit to him. But the truth was, his stomach had been feeling a little queasy.

It had started last night, after the strange phone call from Laurel. She hadn't sounded like herself, and he wished she would have agreed to join them at the ranch rather than hole up in that apartment, all by herself.

The big, noisy family dinner had included some quiet

moments and more than a few tears as they recalled the last time they'd been gathered together—for their brother's funeral.

Corb hadn't been there, of course. He'd still been in the hospital, only one day out of his coma. At that point he hadn't even known his brother was dead.

They'd waited until the day after the funeral to tell him.

So at dinner, he'd listened to his family talk about the service as if he were an outsider. Then later, B.J. had pulled out a DVD of family movies and they managed to have some laughs—and shed more tears—with a trip down memory lane.

The party hadn't wrapped up until after midnight, when Olive finally put her foot down. She'd turned off the music and switched off the lights and everyone had received the message loud and clear and gone to their respective beds.

Alone in his cabin, Corb found he couldn't sleep. He'd missed Sky sleeping in her bed in the corner.

And he missed Laurel.

Too late, he'd wished he'd driven into town like she'd asked him.

He welcomed his chores the next morning, but he couldn't deny that the nervous feeling in his gut just got worse as the day progressed. Now he wondered why he'd bothered putting the food on his plate in the first place. Habit, he supposed. He held out a piece of chicken toward Sky, but even for her favorite food, the loyal dog refused to budge from her spot at Cassidy's feet.

"She's been missing Brock something awful," Corb

told his sister. "I hate to think what she's going to be like when you go back to school."

"I wish I could bring her with me." Cassidy gave Sky's head a good scratch. "But she'd hate apartment living. I'm on the third floor and I don't think she could manage the stairs."

Corb leaned over, dangling the chicken right in front of Sky's nose. Finally she deigned to accept it.

"Did you guys know," Corb asked, "that Sky came from Silver Creek Ranch? She was bred from the same dog that used to belong to our Grandpa Turner."

Grandpa Turner was someone they knew only by name, since he had passed away before they were born.

"That's not true," Cassidy argued. "I found him in a basket at the front door on my fourteenth birthday. Mom was so annoyed, I figured Dad was behind it. And he never would have bought a dog from Maddie Turner. Mom would have killed him."

"I know what you mean," B.J. said. "One of my most vivid memories as a kid is going to town and having Dad walk right by Mom's sister as if he couldn't even see her. That was so not like Dad, I've never forgotten it."

"I have the exact same memory." Corb wondered if maybe he and his brother were remembering the same incident. "Still, I happened to drive up to Silver Creek the other day. Maddie Turner has a couple of border collies the spitting image of Sky. She admitted that Sky was from the same lineage."

"That can't be," Cassidy said again.

"What were you doing driving there, anyway?" B.J. asked.

"The old family feud has been bothering me lately. I noticed Maddie Turner putting a wreath on the road where the car crash happened. It just got me thinking about the fact that we're all related, even though we hardly know her."

"Well, for Mom's sake, I think we better let sleeping dogs lie. Figuratively and literally." B.J. turned to Cassidy. "By the way, is your cell phone charged?"

"Why do you ask?" Cassidy transferred her plate to the coffee table, then pulled her phone out of the front pocket of her jeans. When she saw the blank screen she gave him a puzzled look. "How did you know?"

"Some guy called the house half an hour ago. You must have been in the shower."

"And you're only telling me now?" She scrambled up from the sofa.

"His name was Josh," B.J. teased as she ran off toward her bedroom, with a confused Sky struggling to keep up. No doubt she wanted to plug in her phone and call the guy back, in private. "He sounded really nice. I can't wait to meet him."

"Oh, shut up, B.J.," Cassidy shouted back at him.

Corb smiled. Just like old times.

B.J. leaned back into the sofa. "That girl is starting to worry me," he said. "She's getting way too pretty for her own good."

"I agree. But what about you, bro?" Corb countered. "Any woman in your life right now?"

"Hell, yes. It's all work *and* all play for me on the rodeo circuit. You should have tried in when you had the chance."

"There's enough real cowboy work here on the ranch.

Don't you have enough trophies, belt buckles and prize money by now?"

B.J. looked at him as if he was stupid. "It isn't about the winnings."

"Then what?"

"Not everyone finds Coffee Creek the most wonderful place in the world."

Corb decided to let the conversation end there. He and B.J. had had this same argument before and he never won. Besides, today he had weightier matters on his mind. He carried his plate to the kitchen where he scraped the food into the trash, then placed the plate in the dishwasher.

"Not hungry?" Jackson had been present last night and for most of today, but he kept a low profile and didn't talk much. This morning he and Cassidy had gone out riding for a few hours and he and B.J. had spent some time talking in the tack room afterward.

That was Jackson's way. He preferred to deal with people one-on-one rather than in large groups. Now he was hanging out in the kitchen, looking almost as nerve-racked as Corb felt.

"Big day," Jackson said, his eyes trained on the view out the kitchen window. "You sure Winnie won't be coming to the wedding?"

"Positive. She's just not up to it."

Some of the edge seemed to leave Jackson's face then. "What time is Laurel coming over?"

"The justice of the peace will be here at two-thirty. Laurel and Eugenia will be coming fifteen minutes later." Corb glanced at his watch, surprised to see that it was already past one. "Hell. I better get back to my place and take a shower."

Jackson nodded. "A shave would be a good idea, too."

CORB KNEW IT was supposed to be bad luck for a groom to see the bride before the ceremony on their wedding day. He didn't think there were any rules against talking on the phone, though.

So why wasn't Laurel taking his calls? He'd tried her that morning, after chores, then again after lunch, and once more when he came out of the shower.

All his calls went straight through to messages.

"Where are you, sugar? I hope you slept well. Give me a call when you have a minute."

But either she didn't have a spare minute, or she never checked her messages, because by three o'clock that afternoon he still hadn't heard from her.

The justice of the peace, a friendly woman in her forties who'd driven down from Lewistown and was dressed for the occasion in a light brown suit, had arrived right as scheduled. She was in the kitchen now, sipping tea and chatting with his mother.

Laurel and the others should have been here fifteen minutes ago. Finally, Corb grew tired of pacing the length of the family room and he went out to the yard to wait. Cassidy, Jackson and B.J. came with him.

It was the last day of September. A warm, sunny day that promised only good things.

So where the hell was she?

His stomach knotted as he remembered another wedding when part of the wedding party hadn't arrived on time. Could fate be that cruel? Had she been in an automobile accident?

He could tell other members of his family were anxious, too. Jackson was fiddling with his truck, pretending to check the oil and the tire pressure, all the while keeping one eye on the laneway.

Cassidy and Sky were sitting on the front porch. His sister was wearing the same ivory-colored cowboy boots she'd bought for Winnie and Brock's wedding. At one minute past three, she took them off and flung them angrily in the grass. "Maybe we should call the sheriff."

"No. Hold off. It'll be okay." B.J. was the voice of reason, but Corb could tell that even he was feeling tense. B.J. always went still and calm when he was nervous. A trait he'd either inherited, or picked up from their father.

Then, finally, at five minutes past three, a vehicle came into view. No one relaxed until it was close enough that they could be sure this wasn't an official vehicle, but Eugenia driving an old gray station wagon.

She was alone.

What the hell?

Eugenia was out of the car a second after she turned off the ignition. "I'm so sorry I'm late. I've been trying to call, but maybe someone left the phone off the hook?"

Cassidy came running, barefoot, from the porch. "It's my fault. I unplugged the house phone because I needed to charge my cell. I meant to plug it back in, but I forgot."

Corb waved off her explanation. "Where's Laurel? Is she okay?"

Eugenia's crestfallen expression was not encouraging. She was still wearing an apron, as if she'd left in a hurry.

"I had the food ready to go and stopped to pick up Laurel at two o'clock, just as planned. I was going to help her get into her dress, then drive her here to the ranch."

Corb nodded. Laurel had gone over this with him last Sunday. Which was the last time he'd seen her, he realized, kind of surprised. How had an entire week gone by without them getting together?

"But Laurel wasn't there," Winnie continued. "All her stuff was gone. She left me a note. And this letter for you." She passed Corb an envelope then and he stared at the name written in blue pen on the front.

His name. In Laurel's handwriting.

He folded it in half and tucked it in the back pocket of his pants. He'd have to be someplace private to read it. But first he wanted to know what she'd told Eugenia.

"Did you bring the note she wrote for you?" His voice sounded as though it was coming from someplace faraway. He couldn't believe this was happening to him. Last time they'd made love, he'd thought they were so happy. What had happened to change all that?

And why had Laurel opted to tell him in a letter rather than in person?

She tried last night...you didn't have time.

"I have it," Eugenia said, her gaze traveling to the family members slowly circling around him. Cassidy and Sky on one side, B.J. on the other, Jackson standing slightly behind them all. And then, the only one missing came out of the house.

"Is she finally here?" His mother stepped out of the

house, into the sunshine. She was wearing a dress Corb had never seen before. Her hair had been freshly colored and styled, and she'd put on makeup and proper shoes. Not as gussied up as she'd been for Brock's wedding, but she was mother of the groom—no one would mistake her for anything less.

Not wanting his mother to come to the wrong conclusion, Corb spoke quickly. "It's okay, Mom. Laurel seems to have changed her mind. Eugenia didn't find her at the apartment. But she left a note."

Olive took a few seconds to process all this. Then she pushed her way to the center of her family and stood next to Corb. She sized up Eugenia, then her gaze moved to the note in her hands.

"What did she say?"

Olive sounded fragile, and Corb put a hand around his mother's waist. B.J. moved in closer, too, and Corb wondered why it was that his family never seemed to be able to support one another except in moments of crisis.

Eugenia's hands were shaking as she unfolded the piece of paper.

Eugenia, I'm sorry to do this to you, but I've decided I can't go through with it. Would you please call off the wedding for me? I know I've left this to almost the last possible moment, but I figured this out myself just a few minutes ago.

I've written a letter to Corb explaining everything to him. Please make sure he gets it.

I cleaned the apartment before I left and you'll see I've borrowed Winnie's car to drive to Billings. I'll leave it in the airport parking lot and I'll courier you the keys as soon as I arrive in New York. Please arrange to have someone go and collect it. I'm sorry for the inconvenience. And I'm sorry I won't be there to help with the Cinnamon Stick anymore.

Eugenia stopped. She looked up from the paper to Corb's face. "That's all she wrote. I imagine the rest is in your letter."

He nodded, then turned away and started walking.

"Corb, honey, don't run off." Olive sounded as torn up as he felt. "She never was good enough for you."

Corb kept moving. He headed up Lake Road, his head in a fog.

Suddenly Sky gave a sharp bark. He turned back to look at her. Her eyes fixed right on him, Sky got to her feet, took a few steps in his direction, halted and looked back at Cassidy.

His little sister was crying. She blinked, then nodded at her dog and finally managed to say, "It's okay, Sky. He needs you more. Go."

And Sky went—her lope betraying a slight limp as she advanced toward Corb. When she caught up to him Corb didn't stop but he did pat her briefly on the top of her head. And then they rounded a bend in the road and his family was out of sight.

HE STAYED NUMB for a good while. He'd initially planned to hole up in the sanctuary of his home, but he ended up by the lake, sitting in one of the cedar chairs lining the shore. It was peaceful here. Beautiful. A shimmering upside-down version of the golden aspen, sage-green ponderosa pine and crisp blue sky was reflected in the water.

His camera, safely ensconced in its black case, was sitting on the chair next to his. He'd planned on asking Jackson to take some photographs of the ceremony, which should have happened right here, about fifteen minutes ago now.

Corb sank deeper into his chair. And Sky, faithful Sky, settled patiently at his feet, her head resting over one of his boots.

Time passed. Maybe half an hour.

He started thinking again. Slowly. First he thought of her. Where was she right now? In a plane? Already in New York? What did she look like, how did she feel?

He shifted in his seat then pulled his phone and her letter out from his pockets. First he checked the phone. No missed calls. No messages.

Then he opened the letter. Took a fortifying look at the beauty around him, then started to read.

Dear Corb,

I'm so sorry for canceling our wedding this way. It's cowardly, I know. But I was afraid if I told you in person that you would change my mind. You're a persuasive guy, you know, or at least I find you that way.

Because why else did I agree to this crazy plan of ours? It isn't fair to either of us. You've had such a tough time lately and I know you want to do the right thing, but these are modern times and getting married isn't always the only solution.

We can raise this child without getting married. I know we can make it work.

As for me, I'm not ready to give up my dream of living and working in New York City. So I'm going home. But I will be in touch, and you and I will work out a way for us both to spend time with our child.

Then she signed off. He thought she'd written "Love Laurel" but there was a smear on the word before her name, a little round spot about the size of a teardrop. So maybe she hadn't written love. Maybe it was "best wishes" or something like that.

Corb ran his thumb over her words, trying to imagine her penning this letter in the wee hours of the previous night.

And he'd had no idea. He hadn't even entertained the possibility that she might not show up today.

Now what?

He contemplated the day before him. The week. The month. The year. It all seemed to be just a whole lot of time to get through somehow.

Eventually he remembered his camera. He hadn't used it since before the accident. There were probably pictures on it that he'd taken during the week that he no longer remembered.

Curious, he unzipped the case and pulled out his Nikon. He turned on the power and shifted his body to protect the viewfinder from the sun.

One by one he scrolled through the pictures. There were dozens of them.

And yes, some of them were of Winnie and Brock.

And it hurt to see how happy they were, with no clue of the tragedy that would soon end it all.

But most of the pictures were of Laurel.

He'd clearly been entranced with her. There were pictures she posed for, but even more that he'd taken when she wasn't looking.

One of her crouched next to Sky, rubbing the old dog behind her ears.

Another of her with Winnie, laughing like the life-long friends they were.

And still more of her listening quietly at the dinner table, one with her tucking a strand of her hair behind her ear, and finally a silly shot of her sticking her tongue out at him for taking too many pictures.

At one point he'd wondered if he'd viewed that week as a fun affair with a beautiful woman, or if he'd actually been falling in love.

Looking at all these pictures, the answer was obvious.

There were even some that he must have taken in his bedroom, the night they'd made love, the night she'd become pregnant. She was wearing his shirt—the blue one that had smelled faintly of her perfume. Her hair was long and disheveled and her complexion was pink and her hazel eyes glowed like liquid gold.

He knew that look. There could be no doubt what had happened before those images were captured.

"Wow." He scrolled through the pictures a second time. And a third.

And slowly it hit him. The reason this was hurting so much was because he loved her.

He'd loved her then.

And he loved her now.

More time passed. Eventually Corb heard footsteps approaching from behind. Then his brother handed him a beer, and settled with his own drink in the chair to Corb's right.

"Are you okay?" B.J. stared at the lake, then he turned to Corb, his dark grey eyes full of worry.

"I don't know. I was kind of numb at first. Now I'm starting to feel pretty crappy."

"This came out of the blue? You hadn't fought or anything?"

"No fight." He sighed. "But I can't say it came out of the blue. A few times lately Laurel asked me if I was sure we were doing the right thing. Last night she called and said she wanted to talk. I told her to come to the ranch, but she wanted me to go to her."

"And you didn't."

"I knew Mom would be disappointed…." He stopped and thought about what he'd just said. "Hell."

"Mom is tougher than she looks. You can say no to her now and then and she won't break."

Corb shook his head. "I haven't said no to her at all lately." He'd been trying to be a good son. But every time he'd put his mother first, he'd been putting Laurel second.

Laurel hadn't mentioned anything in her letter about that. She'd made it sound like she'd chosen New York and her career over him.

But he couldn't remember her once talking about her job and how much she missed it.

What he could remember her talking about was his

feelings for Jacqueline. And was he sure they were
doing the right thing?

"This getting married idea was a little rushed," B.J.
said. "Maybe Laurel made the right decision going back
to New York."

Corb wanted to howl. "She's thousands of miles away
from me, man! How can that be the right thing?"

"So, it's more than the baby," B.J. replied, his voice
insufferably calm in the face of Corb's distress. "You
love her."

"I— Yes! I do love her."

"And she knows that?"

Corb didn't answer. Instead, he leaned forward,
wrapping his arms around his head, like it was aching,
when the truth was only his heart was in pain.

"We were talking up at the house, after you left,"
B.J. said.

"I'll bet you were."

"Hey, don't sound bitter. We all want what's best
for you. Mom said something that didn't make sense
to me at the time."

"What else is new?"

B.J. ignored his attempt at a joke. "She said that you
must have done something to scare Laurel off. Mom
said the way that woman looked at you, reminded her
of the way she felt about our father."

Corb sat up straighter. Olive's love for Bob Lambert
was the stuff legends were made of. And his father had
been just as devoted to her.

"When she said that, I thought to myself that she had
to be wrong. If Laurel loved you that much, she'd never
have left. Unless—" He glanced at Corb.

"Unless she didn't know I felt the same way about her." Corb thought with regret of the opportunities he'd had. When he'd asked her to marry him. After they'd made love. On the drive home from buying their wedding rings and the license.

The wasted chances seemed endless now.

"I don't know why I never said those words. I was so focused on the baby, and wanting the kid to grow up in Montana. That's why I asked her to marry me in the first place."

"I guess that's a good reason for some people," B.J. replied. "But it obviously wasn't enough for Laurel."

Chapter Fourteen

It was seven in the evening in New York, which meant it would be five o'clock in Montana. On a regular weekday, Laurel would be closing the café and battling the nausea that always seemed to hit her around this time of day.

So maybe it was pregnancy, and not the swaying and lurching of the taxi as the driver wove through Manhattan traffic, that was making her feel so terrible.

Laurel had brought the barf bag from the plane with her, just in case. She had it close at hand, beside her purse. And if things got much worse, she might need it.

Above her queasy stomach, another one of her internal organs was in pain, too. Her heart felt twice its usual size, as if a heavy weight had been inserted inside.

No pregnancy hormones were to blame for this problem, though. She'd just severed ties with the most amazing man she'd ever known. And what a mess she'd made of it. They'd be calling her the "flyaway bride" back in Coffee Creek. Maybe someone would make a movie. She hoped they got Amy Adams to play her role. Ryan Reynolds could play Corb—only he wasn't nearly cute or sexy enough for the role.

Laurel leaned her head against the windowpane. Everywhere she looked there were buildings and lights, taxis and cars. And people. People out walking their dogs, mothers holding the hand of a child, couples arm in arm, businesspeople striding while talking on the phone or texting, glancing up to orient themselves every now and then.

New York.

Once she'd wanted it so badly. And now it was all hers.

The taxi jerked to a stop. The driver put his arm over the seat and turned so she could see his hawkish profile. "Forty-three dollars."

She had the money ready and passed it to him. "Keep the change."

Her old brown suitcase with the pink ribbon on the handle was in the trunk, but he didn't get out to help her with the luggage, just pressed the button to release the trunk. She unloaded the case to the sidewalk herself, then stood in front of the three-story apartment building where she lived, trying to remember how she'd felt the first time she'd seen it.

Excited and full of hope. Open to adventure, but a little nervous, too.

She wished she could be that girl again, rather than her own nauseous and heartsick self.

Oh, stop feeling sorry for yourself. She gripped her suitcase in one hand, her carry-on and purse in the other and climbed the stairs slowly, planting both feet on one step before heaving the suitcases ahead of her. Her neighbors would think a three-hundred-pound man with mobility issues was on his way up.

The usually musty hallway smelled sweetly of turmeric and coriander. One of her neighbors must be cooking a nice curry for dinner. Laurel set down her cases by the door marked 2C and pulled out her keys.

The place was just as she'd left it, clean and neat, the stale smell almost completely masked by the orange blossom scented infusion sticks she'd left sitting on the table.

She didn't unpack, simply pushed her suitcases against the wall, then looked around the three-hundred-square-foot studio apartment. She'd taken a lot of trouble to decorate the place nicely and make it feel like a real home.

Once she'd thought she'd succeeded.

But now she knew she hadn't. This wasn't her place. Not really. She'd tried New York, and it was exciting and different, but she'd been born in Montana and that was where she truly belonged. Once she'd had a few days to recover and organize she would move to Billings, find a job and rent a bigger apartment—one with room for a baby.

She'd be close to Winnie and also to Corb, who would be able to spend a lot more time with his child than if she chose to stay in New York City.

The decision came to her in a rush, and she was amazed at how right it felt. She'd figured on needing at least a month to figure out the next step in her life.

But now that she knew where she wanted to be, she was anxious to get her plan in motion. First thing was subletting her apartment. She had a good idea who to call.

She dug out her phone, then went to stand by the window as she waited.

"Laurel? Is it really you?" It was her friend Anna from work.

"I'm finally back in the city."

"Oh, good. I've missed you. We all have. The extra work has been insane, even though they hired a temp. Blair was assigned your stories and he's such a pain! He walks around with his nose so high in the air, like he's Anderson Bloody Cooper or something, but his writing totally sucks. Will you be in the office tomorrow?"

She'd forgotten how much Anna liked to talk. But she had to admit it was rather ego-repairing to hear that she'd been missed.

"Actually, I'm not in New York to stay. I've decided to tender my resignation and move back to Montana."

She didn't mention being pregnant. Or her almost-marriage to Corb. What was the point? She and Anna had grown to be pretty good friends in the two years they'd worked at the magazine together. Still, once she moved to Montana, Laurel knew they would eventually drift apart. Not like her and Winnie. No matter what, they were friends for life.

"Seriously?"

"Seriously. I'm here to pack up the rest of my stuff and find someone to sublet my apartment."

Anna sucked in her breath. "Oh—I've always loved your cute little walk-up. And the location! Right by the L train in the East Village."

Laurel smiled, not insulted—well, not much—that Anna was more interested in her studio walk-up than in the fact that she was moving.

"I have nice neighbors, too. And the good news is they have the mouse problem almost under control."

"Very funny." Anna paused. "That was a joke, right?"

"Yes." They made plans to go for dinner on Monday evening to finalize the details. Laurel ended the call feeling curiously empty inside.

She didn't really care about any of it. Not her old job. Not even Anna, that much.

She dropped listlessly to the daybed that also doubled as her couch. She ought to order in some food. Had she eaten anything at all today?

But fatigue caught up to her before she could place another call. She closed her eyes and drifted off....

It was Monday, almost noon, when Corb finally arrived at the address he'd conned out of Winnie without too much difficulty. Getting into the locked main entrance of Laurel's apartment building wasn't difficult. The door was stiff and hadn't closed properly, which meant the lock hadn't caught.

Corb slipped inside. He paused to get his bearings, then, noticing a bank of letter boxes, checked the name for 2C.

Laurel Sheridan. He was definitely at the right place. *Thank you, Winnie.* Her directions had gotten him this far.

The rest was up to him.

He climbed the worn wooden stairs, his boots sounding loudly on each step. When he reached her door, he pulled a paper bag out of his pocket, then knocked.

It took a while for her to come to the door, but he knew she was home, because he could hear sounds.

Footsteps and running water and then suddenly the door opened two inches and he could hear her voice.

"Who's there?"

"Me."

"Corb?" Her voice was a squeak, initially. Then she said a louder and more uncertain, "Corb Lambert?"

"Yup. Would you let me in? I have something of yours."

She closed the door so she could release the safety chain. Then opened it wide and put her hands on her hips, staring at him in disbelief.

She was wearing the same yoga pants and striped shirt that she'd had on the last time he'd dropped by un-announced. Her hair was in the same messy bun, and her eyes had that sleepy, muddled look.

He wanted to kiss her.

But first he'd wait to see if she invited him in.

"How did you get here?"

"Red-eye. A couple of them. I missed a few connections and had to do a little scrambling or I would have been here earlier." He looked past her to the apartment. It looked small. But pretty. Walls were painted a color that looked like fresh butter and there were paintings of flowers on the wall, and cozy rugs on the wooden floors.

"Come in," she said finally.

Three steps put him pretty much in the center of the room. There weren't any bedrooms, just a galley kitchen, a bathroom, and this. Feeling claustrophobic, he went to stand by the window, which was open a few inches.

"So what's in the bag this time?" Laurel asked, crossing her arms over her chest, looking uncomfortable and so damn adorable, all at the same time. "Don't tell me I left my underwear behind again?"

"Not this time." He didn't show her, though. It was too soon. "How are you?"

"I'm okay. Feeling kind of stupid, though. I'm sorry for leaving that way, Corb. I should have talked to you."

"Yeah. You should have."

"And now you've traveled all this way— Oh, I am really sorry, Corb."

Tears shimmered in her eyes. He knew she wasn't crying to make herself more attractive to him, but that was the result just the same. He looked away from her to the street, and the view of the brick building that had been built about six inches from this one.

Why would anyone want a view like this when they could be looking at a lake and mountains and trees?

"I wish you would have talked to me before you left, because there's something I would have told you. Just to see if it made any difference."

She moved closer, as if she could tell how difficult this was for him, and knew that he needed a little encouragement.

"What would you have told me?"

"I would have said that I don't remember falling in love with you the first time." He glanced sideways. Saw her mouth tighten with pain.

"But I *do* remember falling in love with you the second time," he continued. "And I suppose that if somewhere down the line I happened to get another major crack on the head and lost my memory again, I'd fall in love with you a third time, too."

He turned to her then, looking in her eyes for his answer. He was prepared to be shot down. But he knew he had to take this risk rather than spend his life wondering what her answer would have been.

Her eyes were filling with tears again. But he could tell these were the happy kind, and as his heart started lifting, he held out his arms with hope.

And she came to him. Putting her arms around him, too, then laying her head against his chest. "You don't know how badly I wanted to hear you say that."

"I was an idiot. I was hung up on trying to remember the past, not realizing that it was the here and now that mattered most."

"I love you, too, you know. Just in case you were wondering."

"That's nice to hear. Given that you ran off on our wedding day and all."

"I really am sorry about that, Corb."

"It's okay now. I have an apology of my own. I'm sorry I put my mother's preferences about our wedding ahead of yours. Looking back, I can't believe I was so stupid."

"You love your mom. And you're a good son, Corb."

"But I want to be an even better husband." His hand slid down to her belly. "And father."

"You will be. I know it."

He wrapped his arms around her and pulled her in close, wanting no space between them. None at all.

He rested his face against the wild curls on the top of her head. Then he released the clip, setting them free.

She arched her neck back and finally they were kissing. Softly and gently, like two people who still couldn't quite believe this was happening to them.

Eventually he pulled away, needing a little more reassurance. "Does this mean you'll marry me? And come back to Montana?"

"I will," she said solemnly. "I promise."

"And you won't miss the city too much?"

"We can always visit."

"Then it's time you looked in here." He held out the paper bag which had gotten crumpled quite badly while they were kissing.

"It looks empty," she said, but on trust, she slipped her hand inside and felt around.

His heart skipped anxiously when she didn't find anything.

And then her eyes grew wide and her lips parted with a soft "Wow. Oh, Corb."

She pulled out the ring, then passed it to him, holding out her left hand so he could slip it on her finger. It seemed to fit quite well.

"It's beautiful! Corb, where on earth did you get this?"

"They have this store here in New York City. Tiffany's? I told them we wouldn't need the box. We don't, do we?"

"No. Because this ring is never going to leave my finger. I love it, Corb and I'll wear it proudly. But the wedding bands we bought in Lewistown would have been enough."

"No, they wouldn't. I came here to do things right this time, and an engagement ring was part of the package. But I do have a favor to ask of you."

"Anything."

"I'd like to stay a few days and get married here."

"But—I thought you wanted to have our wedding at the ranch. And I do, too. It's so beautiful…it's the perfect place."

"We have our entire lives to enjoy the ranch. Think of the story we can tell our kids, about how I chased you all the way back to New York City, then whisked you off to City Hall to tie the knot."

"That would make a great story," she admitted. "But your mom. She'll be crushed."

"She'll recover. This is *our* day, after all." He pulled her back into his arms, working his hands under her sweatshirt as he leaned in for another kiss. "'Course there are going to be parts of this story we never tell our kids."

She urged him back a few steps, then toppled him down to the daybed with her right on top of him. Her face just inches from his she whispered, "I'd like to get to those parts right now if you don't mind."

He sure didn't.

Epilogue

Seven Months Later

Since her mother-in-law had been denied the wedding she wanted, Laurel graciously allowed her to organize the baby shower.

And Olive, in her own inimitable style, took the ball and ran with it.

B.J. and Cassidy were home for the event, of course. Also invited were all the local ranchers—excluding Maddie Turner, of course—and Vince, Eugenia and Dawn from the café.

Never had the Lambert family been so badly in need of spring as they were this year. Rebirth was all around them. Fields full of sturdy, dark-faced calves and wobbly-legged foals. And best of all, a new baby in the family—two if you counted Winnie's new son, but the Lamberts didn't know about him yet.

None of this made the loss of Brock any easier to handle, but it was a reminder to celebrate the precious gift of life when you could.

Corb felt serenely happy, almost blissful, in the middle of the organized chaos of the event. The house was decorated with fresh tulips and daffodils, as well as balloons in the pastel shades his mother had selected.

Matching napkins and streamers had been purchased in the same watered-down shades—though he'd only noticed this because Laurel had pointed it out to him earlier.

He was holding one-month-old Stephanie in his arms, his gaze following Laurel as she circulated among the guests, sipping sparkling apple juice and turning every now and then to look at him and smile.

He wondered how it was that everyone else in the room wasn't staring at her, too. The only times he could tear his gaze away was when he glanced down at their perfect little daughter, resting against his chest, where he could offer her the warmth and security she needed in the face of all the noise and commotion.

All his life he'd thought his calling in life was to be a rancher. But now he knew it was so much more. Being a husband to Laurel and a father to Stephanie were the roles that meant the most to him. He'd been happy before, but now he felt fulfilled. He knew they were still in the so-called *honeymoon phase* of marriage, but he had no doubt that he and Laurel had what it took to make their relationship last.

Respect, trust…and humor. Somehow even when they were both up at two in the morning dealing with dirty diapers and colic, Laurel could still make him laugh.

She was putting her sense of humor to use in other ways, as well. She'd started a blog a few months before the baby was born. She called it *Rancher's Wife 101* and in it she chronicled the ups of downs of adjusting from life in New York City to being a hands-on wife of a cowboy in Montana, and a new mother to boot.

She had her hands full, that was for sure. But so did they all, and being busy just meant the quiet moments were treasured all the more.

"I see you've found yourself a nice quiet spot here in the corner."

"Busted." He grinned at Vince, the crotchety old baker from the Cinnamon Stick. "Say, I saw you talking to my mother earlier. I didn't know you two were acquainted."

"Oh, we grew up together. I used to know her and her sister real well."

"Maddie."

Vince hesitated, then nodded. "Yes, Maddie."

He slipped off then. Maybe for another soft drink, maybe to get some fresh air.

Corb had been thinking of his aunt more and more lately. In fact, he'd mentioned to Jackson that he was hoping to swing by one day and put on a new roof for her, when Jackson had surprised him and told him he'd handled the job himself.

There were undercurrents in his family that he'd never understand, Corb figured.

Including the whereabouts of Winnie. She still hadn't made it back to Coffee Creek and Laurel refused to discuss this mysterious ailment that apparently wasn't life-threatening, but that also seemed to make travel impossible.

LAUREL WAS MUNCHING down an oatmeal cookie when Cassidy came to join her at the buffet table. The pretty blonde had Stephanie in her arms—and she looked like a natural.

"I can't believe you managed to wrestle her away from Corb." Laurel chased the cookie down with a sip of apple juice. "He'd hold her all day long if he didn't have so much work to do."

"Yeah, I always knew Corb would make a great dad. But I told him he has to share." Cassidy smiled down at the tiny baby snuggled in her arms. "She's so adorable. I wish I didn't have to leave tomorrow."

"Your final exam is next Friday?"

"Yes. And then I'll be done."

"So then what? You know your mother is hoping you'll move back home."

"Oh, right, like I went to all the work of getting my master's so I could work on a ranch for the rest of my life." Cassidy wrinkled her nose. "Sorry. That sounded bitchy. I'm sure I *will* come home for a few weeks at least, just to take a break before I start working full-time."

"That would be nice." Laurel was looking forward to the opportunity to get to know her new sister-in-law a little better. "Do you have a job lined up?"

Anxiety creased Cassidy's fine brow. "I have a few prospects, but no firm offers."

Laurel touched her arm sympathetically. "Give it time. I'm sure the offers will come soon enough."

The baby's eyes suddenly popped open. She gazed up at Cassidy with a worried frown on her forehead.

"What's the matter, sweetie? Don't recognize me?"

Despite Cassidy's loving tone, the baby started to

cry, and Laurel happily helped Cassidy transfer the bundle to her.

"Stephanie is such a pretty name."

"We named her after my mother," Laurel explained. After both mothers, actually. She hoped her daughter didn't one day complain about the middle name Olive. But it would have been impolitic not to include both grandmothers as namesakes.

Corb joined them then, slipping an arm over Laurel's shoulders, then bending over to give his little girl a kiss.

"You two are sickeningly happy," Cassidy said, the harsh words tempered with a reluctant smile.

"Maybe one day you'll be so lucky," Corb replied mildly.

"I doubt it."

"What about that Josh fellow? You still seeing him? Farley will be pretty disappointed if you are."

"Isn't Farley the vet?" Laurel had been following the banter up to that point. Now she gave Corb a look of total confusion.

But Cassidy had no trouble deciphering his meaning. "Stop it, Corb. You're supposed to be the nice brother, remember?" Face flushed and eyes bright, she turned and disappeared into the crowd.

"What was that about?" Laurel asked her husband, leaning a little against his solid chest.

"It's a long story." Corb nuzzled the side of her neck. "Is this party going to break up soon? I want to take my girls home. I'm tired of sharing."

Laurel smiled, more to herself than anything. She was so, so lucky to have found this man.

And this family, too. For the most part, she was enjoying being a new member of the Lambert clan. Once she'd been an orphan with no siblings or extended family. Now she had, not only a husband, a daughter and the best friend in the world, but also two new brothers and a sister, as well.

Plus a mother-in-law, of course. Olive was a challenge but the new baby had softened her. Hopefully the changes would be permanent.

And if they weren't, Laurel wouldn't complain. She'd never expected perfection. But here, in Coffee Creek, Montana, she'd come darn close.

* * * * *

Look for C.J. Carmichael's next book in her
COFFEE CREEK, MONTANA *series,*
HER COWBOY DILEMMA, when
Cassidy Lambert finally meets her match!
Available in April 2013 wherever
Harlequin books are sold.

COMING NEXT MONTH
from Harlequin® American Romance®

AVAILABLE FEBRUARY 5, 2013

#1437 THE TEXAS RANCHER'S FAMILY
Legends of Laramie County
Cathy Gillen Thacker
Mac Wheeler wants to bring his clean-energy plan to Texas but runs into opposition from Erin Monroe. She doesn't want to sell her ranch—no matter how persuasive Mac may be!

#1438 MY COWBOY VALENTINE
2 stories in 1!
Jane Porter and Tanya Michaels
Two Texas cowboys in two Valentine stories by two great authors: "Be Mine, Cowboy" by Jane Porter and "Hill Country Cupid" by Tanya Michaels. Better than a box of chocolates!

#1439 SWEET HOME COLORADO
The O'Malley Men
by C.C. Coburn
Grace Saunders has returned to Spruce Lake to renovate a house, not rekindle a romance with contractor Jack O'Malley. But can they ignore their attraction—and should Grace reveal a long-buried secret?

#1440 THE ALASKAN RESCUE
Dominique Burton
When Sashi Hansen finds herself in trouble in the wilds of Alaska, Dr. Cole Stevens comes to her rescue. Does he look at her as just a patient—or do they share the same intense desire?

You can find more information on upcoming Harlequin®
titles, free excerpts and more at www.Harlequin.com.

HARCNM0113

REQUEST YOUR FREE BOOKS!
2 FREE NOVELS PLUS 2 *FREE GIFTS!*

HARLEQUIN®

American ★ Romance®

LOVE, HOME & HAPPINESS

YES! Please send me 2 FREE Harlequin® American Romance® novels and my 2 FREE gifts (gifts are worth about $10). After receiving them, if I don't wish to receive any more books, I can return the shipping statement marked "cancel." If I don't cancel, I will receive 4 brand-new novels every month and be billed just $4.49 per book in the U.S. or $5.24 per book in Canada. That's a savings of at least 14% off the cover price! It's quite a bargain! Shipping and handling is just 50¢ per book in the U.S. and 75¢ per book in Canada.* I understand that accepting the 2 free books and gifts places me under no obligation to buy anything. I can always return a shipment and cancel at any time. Even if I never buy another book, the two free books and gifts are mine to keep forever.

154/354 HDN FVPK

Name	(PLEASE PRINT)

Address	Apt. #

City	State/Prov.	Zip/Postal Code

Signature (if under 18, a parent or guardian must sign)

Mail to the **Harlequin® Reader Service:**
IN U.S.A.: P.O. Box 1867, Buffalo, NY 14240-1867
IN CANADA: P.O. Box 609, Fort Erie, Ontario L2A 5X3

Want to try two free books from another line?
Call 1-800-873-8635 or visit www.ReaderService.com.

* Terms and prices subject to change without notice. Prices do not include applicable taxes. Sales tax applicable in N.Y. Canadian residents will be charged applicable taxes. Offer not valid in Quebec. This offer is limited to one order per household. Not valid for current subscribers to Harlequin American Romance books. All orders subject to credit approval. Credit or debit balances in a customer's account(s) may be offset by any other outstanding balance owed by or to the customer. Please allow 4 to 6 weeks for delivery. Offer available while quantities last.

Your Privacy—The Harlequin® Reader Service is committed to protecting your privacy. Our Privacy Policy is available online at www.ReaderService.com or upon request from the Harlequin Reader Service.

We make a portion of our mailing list available to reputable third parties that offer products we believe may interest you. If you prefer that we not exchange your name with third parties, or if you wish to clarify or modify your communication preferences, please visit us at www.ReaderService.com/consumerschoice or write to us at Harlequin Reader Service Preference Service, P.O. Box 9062, Buffalo, NY 14269. Include your complete name and address.

HAR13

Wild for the Sheriff

by Kathleen O'Brien

On sale February 5

Dallas Garwood has always been the good
guy, the one who does the right thing...except
whenever he crosses paths with
Rowena Wright. Now that she's back, things
could get interesting for this small-town sheriff!
Read on for an exciting excerpt from
Wild for the Sheriff by Kathleen O'Brien.

Dallas Garwood had always known that sooner or later he'd
open a door, turn a corner or look up from his desk and see
Rowena Wright standing there.

It wasn't logical. It was simply an unshakable certainty that
she wasn't gone for good, that one day she would return.

Not to see him, of course. He didn't kid himself that their
brief interlude had been important to her. But she'd be back
for Bell River—the ranch that was part of her.

Still, he hadn't thought today would be the day he'd face her
across the threshold of her former home.

Or that she would look so gaunt. Her beauty was still there,
but buried beneath some kind of haggard exhaustion. Her
wild green eyes were circled with shadows, and her white shirt
and jeans hung on her.

Something twisted in his chest, stealing his words. He'd never expected to feel pity for Rowena Wright.

She still knew how to look sardonic. She took him in, and he saw himself as she did, from the white-lightning scar dividing his right eyebrow to the shiny gold star pinned at his breast.

Three-tenths of a second. That was all it took to make him feel boring and overdressed, as if his uniform were as much a costume as his son Alec's cowboy hat.

"*Sheriff* Dallas Garwood." The crooked smile on her red lips was cryptic. "I should have known. Truly, I should have known."

"I didn't realize you'd come home," he said, wishing he didn't sound so stiff.

"Come *back*," she corrected him. "After all these years, it might be a bit of a stretch to call Bell River *home*."

"I see." He didn't really, but so what? He'd been her lover once, but never her friend.

The funny thing was, right now he'd give almost anything to change that and resurrect that long-ago connection.

Will Dallas and Rowena reconnect? Or will she skip town again with everything left unsaid? Find out in *Wild for the Sheriff* by Kathleen O'Brien, available February 2013 from Harlequin® Superromance®.